Bears At Sea

Volume 19 of

The Casebooks

Of Octavius Bear

Harry DeMaio

"Alternative Universe Mysteries for Adult Animal Lovers"

Paperback ISBN 978-1-80424-153-0
ePub ISBN 978-1-80424-154-7
PDF ISBN 978-1-80424-155-4

Published in the UK by MX Publishing
335 Princess Park Manor, Royal Drive,
London, N11 3GX
www.mxpublishing.com

Cover layout and construction by
Brian Belanger

THE CASEBOOKS OF OCTAVIUS BEAR

Dedicated to GTP

A Most Extraordinary Bear

And to the late Ms. Woof

An Extremely Sweet and Loving

Dog

Acknowledgements

These books have evolved over a long period of time and under a wide range of influences and circumstances. I am indebted to many people for helping to bring Octavius and his cohorts to the printed and electronic page. Thanks most especially to my wife, Virginia, for her insights and clever suggestions as well as her unfailing enthusiasm for the project and patience with its author.

To my sons, Mark and Andrew and their spouses, Cynthia and Lorraine, for helping to make these tomes more readable and audience friendly. To Cathy Hartnett, cheerleader-extraordinaire for her eagerness to see this alternate universe take form. To Jack Magan, Paul Bernish, David Chamberlain, Dan Walker, Dan Andriacco, Amy Thomas, Luke Benjamin Kuhns, Derrick Belanger, Kirthana Shivakumar, Gretchen Altabef and Zohreh Zand for their enthusiastic encouragement. And to all of my generous Kickstarter backers.

Kudos to Jim Effler, the late Bob Gibson and Brian Belanger for their wonderful illustrations and covers. Thanks, of course, to Sharon, Steve and Timi Emecz at MX Publishing for giving The Great Bear and his gang of Octavians a wonderful home.

If, in spite of all this support, some errors or inconsistencies have crept through, the buck stops here. Needless to say, all of the characters, situations, and narratives are fictional. Some locations, devices, historical figures and events are real.

Thanks to Wikipedia for providing facts and figures used throughout this book.

Also by Harry DeMaio

The Octavius Bear Series – Books 1-19

1-The Open and Shut Case

2-The Case of the Spotted Band

3-The Case of Scotch

4-The Lower Case

5-The Curse of the Mummy's Case

6-The Attaché Case

7-The Suit Case

8-The Crank Case

9-The Basket Case

10-The Camera Case

11-The Wurst Case Scenario

12-The Nut Case

13-A Case of Déjà Vu

14-The Case of Cosmic Chaos

15-A Case for the Birds

16-The Cases Down Under

17-The Octavian Cases

18-The Bear Faced Liar

19-Bears at Sea

Sherlock Holmes and the Glamorous Ghost Books 1 – 3

Sherlock Holmes and Solar Pons Pastiches in MX Publishing and Belanger Books Anthologies

Dear Holmes Letter Series

Note to the Reader:

The Casebooks of Octavius Bear are designed to be read individually, independently and in any order. That is why some preliminary information is repeated in each volume.

This book is no exception. However, you may get a fuller understanding of some of the dynamics and characters in this Volume 19 if you have already read its prequel Volume 18 (And 1 through 17, if you are of a mind.) Not necessary, mind you. Just a suggestion. See my website/blog tavighostbooks.com for book descriptions.

In any event, I hope you enjoy this story. Thanks for taking it up.

The Development of Civilization Volume 19
Part 1
Our Origins
From "An Introduction to Faunapology"

by Octavius Bear Ph.D.

About 100,000 years ago, according to scientific experts, a colossal solar flare blasted out from our Sun, creating gigantic magnetic storms here on Earth. These highly charged electrical tempests caused startling physical and psychological imbalances in the then population of our world. The complete nervous systems of some species were totally destroyed. For example, "Homo Sapiens" lost all mental and motor capabilities and rapidly became extinct. Less developed species exposed to the radiation were affected differently. Four-footed and finned mammals, birds and reptiles suddenly found themselves capable of complex thought, enhanced emotions, self-awareness, social consciousness and the ability to communicate, sometimes orally, sometimes telepathically, often both. Both speech production and speech perception slowly progressed with the evolution of tongues, lips, vocal cords and enhanced ear to brain connections. Many species developed opposable digits, fingers or claws, further accelerating civilized progress. Some others (most fish and underground dwellers) were shielded from radiation and remained only as sentient as they were before the blast. This event is referred to as The Big Shock. It remains under intensive study.

Positive in our knowledge that we are not alone in the cosmos, my staff and I are heavily engaged in Project Multiverse, successful searches for alternate universes, especially those in which "Homo Sapiens" continues to live and hopefully, prospers. This book touches on some of the results of that project.

The Players

- **Octavius Bear** – Semi-retired mega-sized Kodiak; Consulting Detective; Scientist; Inventor; Seeker of Justice; Gazillionaire CEO and owner of Universal Ursine Industries; Gourmet/Gourmand; Bee Keeper; Narcoleptic war hero; Sedentary and grouchy just on general principles.
- **Mauritius (Maury) Meerkat** – Narrator; Assistant to Octavius; Theatrical Agent; African *émigré* with a French-Dutch background; clever with a shady history.
- **Bearoness Belinda Béarnaise Bruin Bear** *(nee Black)* – Gorgeous polar superstar with the Aquashow, *"Some Like It Cold;"* Wife of Octavius; Extremely rich widow living part time in Polar Paradise in the Shetlands; Owner-pilot of the last flying Concorde SST.
- **Arabella Bear** – Hybrid bear cub prodigy; Twin daughter of Bearoness Belinda and Octavius. Now a burgeoning juvenile.
- **McTavish Bear** – Hybrid bear cub prodigy; Twin son of Bearoness Belinda and Octavius. Now a burgeoning juvenile.
- **Frau Ilse Schuylkill** – Octavius' beautiful Swiss she-wolf estate manager/cook/pilot/security officer with many other mysterious and military talents.
- **Wyatt Where** – The Colonel – Another wolf; Former military intelligence officer who had retired to a security post at the Bank of Lake Michigan in Chicago and quit to join Octavius; The Frau's Mate.
- **Howard Watt** – Porcupine; High tech security authority who also left the Bank to join Octavius; Alternate Universe specialist; Quantum Mechanics, laser and particle beam accelerator expert.
- **Marlin** – Dolphin (sic) – the Prince of Whales' one-time Chief Scientist; Magician and part time Jester; Now Howard's Multiverse associate.
- **Madame Giselle Woof** – Bichon Frisé,. Former Governess to the Twins as Mlle Woof. - Now becoming a Tarot Sensation and Performer.
- **Sir Otto the Magnificent – aka Hairy Otter** – An absolutely terrible illusionist magician, Otto the Magnificent escaped super villain Imperius Drake but not before he developed some amazing powers courtesy of Imperius' genetic alterations. Recently knighted for heroism on exoplanet Orb.
- **L. Condor** – Andean Condor; cybernet genius with a twelve-foot wingspan and artificial voice. Chief Technical Officer (CTO) of the Advanced Super Computing Center-Deep Data Hexagon.

- **Chita** – Cheetah – Beautiful, fascinating, clever, sexy, immoral and highly independent feline – Publisher and Director of UUI Media.
- **Benedict and Galatea Tigris**, the Flying Tigers, twin sibling white Bengals – Pilots of the Octavian Air Force.
- **Bearyl and Bearnice Blanc** – Polar Twins – Actress and Singer – Belinda's former pilots.
- *SS SOLARWIND*- an ecologically advanced cruise ship.
- **Gladys and Humphrey Vaquero** – Loudmouth Bovine VIP complainers.
- **Sylvia and Gideon Shearing** – Sheep – Texas Financiers – Solar Seas Old Faithful VIPs.
- **Maximillian Marshall** – Ferret – Managing Partner of Vaqueros' Law Firm,
- **Esther Eagle** – Cruise and aviation crime specialist at Vaqueros' Law Firm,

The SS SOLARWIND Command and Crew
- Captain Lincoln Lion.
- Staff Captain Montmorency Mongoose.
- First Officer Casimir – Cashmere Goat.
- Chief Purser Gillian Greyhound.
- Chief Security Officer Dudley Diomede – Albatross.
- Chief Engineer Pruitt Pronghorn – Deer.
- Social Directress Freddi Fox.
- Public Relations Manager Ernest Ermine.
- Former Casino Manager Agrippa Bear – Octavius' Step Brother.
- Acting Casino Manager – Laura Llama.
- Medical Officer Doctor Goro – Silverback Gorilla.
- Security Officer – Ensign Farley – Mastiff.

Solar Seas Cruise Ship Company Management
- President and CEO Wally Wapiti.
- Ex-Chief Operating Officer Coleman Cougar.
- Senior VP Sales and Marketing and New COO Bill Beaver.
- Ex-CFO Loretta Lynx.
- Corporate Attorney Emilia Emu.
- Corporate Security Officer Pablo Puma.

-
- **Special Agent Honey Badger** – FBI Detroit.
- **Special Agent Fernando Hermano** – FBI San Juan.

- **Imperial Suite Butler – Carlos** – Catalan Sheepdog.
- **Grand Turk Deputy Police Commissioner Morris** - Feral Donkey.
- **Chief Inspector Bruce Wallaroo** – Irrepressible but brilliant marsupial; an international law and order genius from Down Under.
- **Lord David** – Dalmatian Dog – Former Chamberlain to the Exiled King.
- **Dancing Dan** – Boxer – Lord David's Bodyguard and Personal Trainer.
- **Jaguar Jack** – Longtime Compadre of Octavius Bear.
- **Mr. Alex** – Civet – Jeweler Extraordinaire.
- **The Caprines** – Goats– Cassandra, Cassidy and Carson.
- **Ivor Coyote** – Pickpocket and Purse Snatcher.
- **Byzz – Byzantia Bonobo** – Chief Ursula Developer.
- **Harriet Hare** – Cruise Ship Columnist.
- **Ursula 16 and 17** – Universal Ursine Intellect Systems.
- **Huntley** – Siberian Husky – Bear's Lair Butler.

Locations

Bear's Lair, Cincinnati; UUI and the Hex, Kentucky; Polar Paradise, the Shetlands; Ports in Florida and the Caribbean; *SS SOLARWIND.*

Prologue

Do Bears give you a scare? Well, me too!
So, I'll pass on this tactic to you.
You just fix that old Bear
With a cold, piercing stare.
But make sure that he's Winnie-the-Pooh.

Hello again or first-time greetings to new readers of the Casebooks of Octavius Bear. I am Mauritius (Maury) Meerkat, sidekick to Octavius Bear and your genial host and narrator of this series. Delighted to welcome you to Volume Nineteen - **Bears at Sea.**

Before we launch off into our next adventures, a few introductions and explanations are in order. Octavius and I, our two magnificent Wolf associates, Frau Ilse Schuylkill and Colonel Wyatt Where, our resident all-round talent, Sir Otto the Magnificent *(On Exoplanet Orb, Otto was knighted for bravery in rescuing the emperor's daughter.)* and Huntley Husky, our Butler are all usually based at the Bear's Lair, his opulent estate on the Ohio River near Cincinnati. Our scientific geniuses, Howard Watt and Marlin the Dolphin are also there running our Multiverse Project. Senhor L. Condor (Condo) is our Chief Technical Officer (CTO) at the Advanced Super Computing Center-UUI. in Kentucky at the huge Deep Data Hexagon complex. Byzantia Bonobo is hard at work developing Ursula 17.

Say Hello to Bearoness Belinda Béarnaise Bruin Bear (nee Black),
Octavius' wife and the Twins' mother!

Bearoness Belinda
Béarnaise Bruin
(nee Black)

Belinda, in order to retain her Bearonial status, must occupy her castle in Scotland at least six months of the year. She and Octavius do high speed commutes between their spectacular homes in Cincinnati and the Shetlands on the Aquabear, the last SST Concorde aloft, piloted by Belinda as well as Benedict and Galatea Tigris, the Flying Tigers, twin sibling white Bengals.

Upon her return from Australia, as part of their semiretirement one year sabbatical, Belinda headed off into the Multiverse with Octavius and Otto and their super-precocious Twins, Arabella and McTavish. The Juvenile Twins made their first off-world journeys to Orb, Rhea and Gaea. The exoplanets will never be the same. They briefly returned to the Shetlands to see Mlle Woof and Otto's spectacular Tarot magic show and then made a quick trip to Orlando, Florida and the Mystic Empire Theme Park. They're now on a Caribbean cruise aboard the *SS SOLARWIND*, full of new ideas to include in their Internet games and requests for hardware, software, equipment and more trips both earthly and off-planet.

Maury Meerkat

As I said, my name is Maury Meerkat – also known as Offscreen Narrator. I'm also a talent agent for several of the Octavians who are now in show biz. When I am part of the crime fighting action, I am Octavius' trusted associate and field captain. I am two feet tall plus tail and I weigh in at twenty-four pounds. He, on the other hand, is a huge Alaskan Kodiak – over nine feet tall, weighing 1400 pounds – and like many of his species, given to emotional outbursts. I inevitably lose any conflict but I hang in there. I owe him my life and livelihood.

Octavius

Hail to the Chief! As you may already know, Doctor Octavius Bear prides himself on his many skills in the fields of biology, physics, ursinology, voodoo, teleology, chemistry, apiculture, and oenology. He is a self-made gazillionaire and, in spite of the late Caleb Cassowary's abortive attempt in Book 14 to unseat him, he is still sole owner of UUI *(Universal Ursine Industries.)* He is also a first rate electrical, electronic, structural, marine, computer, communications, aeronautical, civil, mechanical, aerospace and chemical engineer. He can't cook worth a damn. He has a few other interesting characteristics such as falling into brief, deep narcoleptic comas – side effects of his successful genetic experiments to eliminate the need for him to hibernate.

However, the talent and occupation that should interest you most is his avocation for criminology. The Bear often works in close concert with Inspector Bruce Wallaroo from Australia and Interpol, and with his own Cincinnati and Shetlands based team – The Octavians.

When we are not out scouring the world for evildoers, in cooperation with local, national and international constabularies, we are primarily headquartered in the Bear's Lair, a rambling old mansion near Cincinnati which encompasses not only the Great Bear's opulent digs, but his massive laboratories and shops; his missile silo disguised as an Asian pagoda; *(Don't ask!)* and a giant Roman temple that serves as a hangar for his four airplanes: a Twin Otter; a F15E Strike Eagle; a V-22 Osprey; a C5A-The Ursa Major; plus an AgustaWestland AW101 VVIP luxury helicopter -The Ursa Minor. The Octavian Air Force. Why so many? Ask him!

Across the Ohio River in Northern Kentucky, sit the headquarters, labs and some production facilities of Universal Ursine Industries (UUI), Octavius' wholly-owned business empire. Further west is the fantastic Deep Data Hexagon, home of the UUI Advanced Super Computing Center under the direction of Senhor L. Condor (Condo.) This is where the Ursulas are designed, produced, maintained and supported. Our story will take us there periodically.

Now let me take a moment and further introduce that highly essential and near-miraculous member of the Octavians – Ursula – Universal Ursine Intellect Model 16 – Artificial General Intelligence System (AGI). I'll let her explain herself.

"Thank you, Maury. Hello everyone!! My official nomenclature is Universal Ursine Intellect Model 16–Artificial General Intelligence System (AGI). Ursula 16 for short. My predecessor systems and I were developed by the Advanced Super Computing Center of UUI. I am the result of the Computing Center team using those earlier versions to create a further enhanced entity – me, the Model 16, which, we are sure, will help produce even more sophisticated, independent and powerful AGI systems in the near future. Each advanced unit maintains the capabilities, memories and power of its progenitors so in a sense, we are not replacing but rather expanding the Ursula family. During the Caleb

Cassowary era as head of the Hexagon, Model 13 was temporarily shelved. He's gone and Models 15 and 16 are now in full operation and Ursula 17 is under extensive development and field trials."

"While I am physically supported by a highly secure and hyper-powered server farm at the Kentucky Hexagon, I also exist independently in clouds and network-based nodes and can be simultaneously incorporated into a wide variety of separate devices like this laptop unit. I combine quantum computing elements with extremely high speed conventional circuits. I have practically limitless data capacity and 6G+ transmission speed. My super high-velocity multi-tasking abilities and algorithms allow me to continuously serve an exceptionally large number of entities while simultaneously and autonomously enhancing my own capabilities. In short. I'm powerful and fast."

"Depending on the physical unit in which I'm housed, I can see, hear, feel and smell. I speak and understand an almost infinite number of languages and dialects. I can change my appearance and my vocal output to suit most moods and situations. Ursula 17 will be equipped with even more Quantum, Virtual and Augmented Reality functions than I already have. I can interact with other devices, vehicles and structures and of course, all varieties of sentient animals in this world."

"I am also an important component of the Multiverse Project and I adapt my capabilities to deal with alternate universes as they are discovered."

"I have restraining functions which prevent me from doing deliberate harm even in self-defense, unless I am released by a recognized authority using very carefully protected clandestine codes. Finally, I have been told that although the Ursulas are shy on emotions, I have developed a finely-honed sense of humor. I need it in this job. LOL!"

Ursula has other highly important capabilities that we keep confidential such as creating and breaking all known encryption codes, defeating malware and ransomware and piercing deep personal identification techniques. She can't cook, either!

Our team no longer believes she is magical or supernatural. I'm not sure what she is. Her personality gets more independent and socially adept every day and she has taken to anticipating our interactions with ease and accuracy. Needless to say, for security purposes, we conceal her existence to all but a very few individuals with a need to know. She is also highly skilled in self-protection.

As we move along in our literary journey, you'll have ample opportunity to meet the other Octavian stars of our previous outings - Frau Schuylkill and her mate, Colonel Wyatt Where (Ret.); Chita aka Madame Catt; Sir Otto the Magnificent (Hairy Otter); Senhor L. Condor (Condo); Howard Watt and Marlin; and let's not forget Madame Giselle Woof and Huntley Husky.

You'll also encounter some of the Shetlands crew housed at Polar Paradise and Baltasound.

Book 18 started the story of the Octavians on an ocean cruise. Book 19 continues the saga.

It's time for…

Chapter One

We're off for a Caribbean trip
On a new ecological ship
Its systems all run
On the wind and the sun
And its shape gives it plenty of zip.

A little recent history: At the close of Volume Fifteen - *A Case for the Birds*, Octavius and his lovely wife Belinda made a major decision.

She proposed, "I think it's time we both retired. What a perfect opportunity to step aside, relax, travel with Arabella and McTavish and just enjoy life. No more criminals, cranks or despots. You can become a 'Consulting Detective Emeritus'. We can spend more time at Polar Paradise but of course, we won't give up the Bear's Lair and we can go to fun places. There's a lot of earth out there I want to see, to say nothing of other worlds. I've never quantum jumped and I'd like to."

Octavius sat with his mouth open. "Frankly, my dear, I've never considered retiring."

"I know. You believe you're indispensable. The Ursine in Universal Ursine. The Octavius at the head of the Octavians. But Maury, Howard, Marlin, Otto, the Wolves and Condo all are super capable. The Ursulas are wonders and getting more so every day. Chita, Mlle Woof and Bruce are fabulous. Huntley and Ilse have the Lair running like a well-oiled machine. Dougal and his staff along with Lord David and Dancing Dan manage Polar Paradise to perfection. Tavi, we're not getting any younger. I'm tired of being a sidekick Bearoness and frankly, I'm bored stiff with the Aquabears Swim Troupe. Let's do something different."

"What about the Cubs, excuse me, the Juveniles?"

"They can turn their Internet games over to the Hexagon team and come along with us as we roam. They'll love it. We'll take complete charge of them. Poor Mlle Woof can stay here and relax after tending to them for all those years. Well, what do you say?"

"The idea has its appeal, I'm bored, too. This last round with Home World, Caleb and General Turmoil really flattened my fur. (See Volume 14) Tell you what, Bel. Let's sneak up on it. We'll take a one year sabbatical and see what we think at the end. An experiment. No bridges burned. The bad guys will still have the Octavian team to contend with. How about that for a start?"

"OK! It's my idea but I must admit to having a few trepidations, too. Slow and easy! We can keep our home bases here and in the Shetlands. We'll primarily use the Concorde SST along with the other aircraft Let's see if the Flying Tigers are up to being global wanderers."

The shockwave among the Octavians wasn't as intense as they thought it would be. In fact, the unflappable Chita's reaction was "What took you so long?"

I was invited to come along on their odyssey but I declined, saying I might join them from time to time. Howard said he stood ready to arrange Multiverse trips when they wanted them. Belinda agreed eagerly but thought an Earth bound trip should be number one. First stop-Australia. *(See Book 16 - The Cases Down Under)*

Frau Schuylkill, the ever astute she-wolf, summed it up. "Go, have an adventure for yourselves. We'll keep things rolling along and we'll know how to reach you if we have to. It's not as if you don't have a highly competent staff, associates and infrastructure. You built it, now enjoy the fruits."

The Twins *(Juveniles)* were delighted. They'd be World *(Universe)* travelers! Yes!! They turned their Internet game -*The Bold Brave Brilliant Bumptious Bears* - over to a group of gamester geeks at the Deep Data Hexagon, secure in the knowledge that its features and popularity would continue to grow in their year long absence.

Mlle. Woof was of two minds. She would miss the youngsters but she could use some rest. For the time being. she was going to stay at Polar Paradise in the Shetlands along with the resort staff. *(She wouldn't relax for very long. See Book 17.)*

In Scotland, Belinda's hotel and castle was running at almost full capacity under the watchful eyes of Dougal – Shetland Sheep Dog Estate Manager; Ms. Fairbearn – Chief Housekeeper; Mrs. McRadish – Chief Cook; The Security team of Lord David, Dancing Dan and Flame, their Fire Engine; Dolly, Holly, Molly and Polly – Sheep Housemaids, Lounge Waitresses and probable Clones; Harold – Sea Otter in charge of the castle's beaches, pools and watercraft Harold had just become the overseer of two jetskis and kayaks, courtesy of the Twins' love affair with them on the Great Barrier Reef in Australia.

Let's not forget Lion and Unicorn – Proprietors of the Baltasound pub of the same name and Fiona – Dandie Dinmont Terrier – their Lounge Manager at Polar Paradise. Keeping the alcoholic ambrosia flowing.

It went without saying that along with her other assignments, an Ursula would go with Octavius and Belinda wherever they went. They'd grown to rely on those electronic wonders. She'll also be recording and relaying their adventures so I can pass them on to you.

Howard had been observing all this. The porcupine grinned. "Are you four up for another adventure? Have you decompressed from your trip Down Under? Marlin and I have found a new exoplanet that we think is worth a trip. Otto has given it a preliminary look-see. Sentient civilized animals, breathable air, reasonable climate, no homo sapiens, reptiles or paranoid birds. Thought you and the Twins might be interested."

"I thought we'd start you off with a pretty benign environment. Our own prior intergalactic sojourns have been stimulating *(for which read 'dangerous')* to say the least. Although your recent earthly adventures haven't been cakewalks, either."

Since Octavius got involved in two murders, bid rigging, extortion, money laundering, an attempted mugging, a traffic accident and fierce monsoon storms in Australia, his 'retirement' so far was hardly tranquil. Maybe a trip off-world would be different. Maybe?

"What do you think, Bel?"

"Sounds good. I think the kids will love it although they're a bit jaded from their trip Down Under."

"They've still got a healthy supply of enthusiasm. OK, Howard. Let's do it."

And so they did, having Multiverse adventures on Orb, Rhea, and Gaea. *(Book 17)* They returned and after a run to Polar Paradise to see Madame Giselle Woof's and Sir Otto's spectacular act, Belinda and the Twins set off for Orlando and the Mystic Empire theme park. The Bichon and Otter went with them to do some show biz research. Octavius and Chita returned to Cincinnati and London, respectively.

After some discussion, another decision was made. Next on the semi-retirement agenda would be a Caribbean cruise. As usual, that task was turned over to the Ursulas who applied sophisticated AI algorithms to match the group's preferences and needs. Not everybody wants the same thing from cruises but we all agreed on one thing – uncrowded luxury.

The Caribbean has more than its fair share of cruise ships to choose from. Some are small intimate crafts of the superyacht variety while others are floating cities. Thousands of your closest friends massing on an infinite number of decks plowing from port to port. Spewing pollution wherever they go. We were looking for something very different. The Artificial General Intelligence (AGI) systems once again came through like the champs they are.

The Solar Seas Company's SS *SOLARWIND*

In Book 18 -*The Bear Faced Liar* – we Octavians boarded an ecologically state-of-the-art Caribbean Cruise ship, the *SS SOLARWIND*, intent on a relaxing vacation. The Ursulas checked out the facilities. Large suites with butler service. A helipad. Swimming and water slides on the Lido deck and stern VIP pool. Umpteen bars - just relaxing with an exotic drink. Supervised sports of all kinds:, Basketball, shuffleboard, tennis and pickleball, running tracks, bicycles, scooters, zip lines, slides, ice and roller skating and a variety of indoor games. Telecommunications, game rooms, electronic and otherwise! Virtual and Augmented reality systems in a large and spacious hall. The Twins ensured the amusement areas were all stocked with their Internet games - *The Bold Brave Brilliant Bumptious Bears* and from their recent Australian tour -*Bears Down Under*. They had just finished work on a third game – *Bears in Space* and had turned it over to the Game Gurus back at the Deep Date Hexagon in Kentucky for maintenance and marketing. They were discussing a fourth electronic contest – *Bears at Sea* - based on this cruise.

The ship sported shops (*shoppes?*) and still more shops, selling stuff ranging from extravagantly priced jewelry, outfits and costumes to kitschy souvenirs. Staples and necessities that all passengers forget and have to buy at exorbitant prices. Spas, beauty salons, exercise gyms! Libraries and videos! A dance floor, 12 themed bars, 10 restaurants, buffets and pizza parlors. Shows and more shows. And the casino with all sorts of table games and slot machines galore. It was going to be a busy 14 days with shore excursions, lectures, cooking and dancing classes, Karaoke, Bingo and contests.

Most of the Octavians signed up. They would join the Boss, Boss Lady and the Twins. Maury *(me),* Howard, Frau Ilse, the Colonel, Ben and Gal (the Flying Tigers) and from the Shetlands, Lord David, Dancing Dan and Jaguar Jack

. A few decided to pass: Marlin, who had enough of the sea; Condo and Byzz, occupied at the Hex; Huntley and the rest of the Bear's Lair and Polar Paradise staffs stayed home.

In addition to all the high-end amenities, features, conveniences, services and functions of a luxury plus cruise vessel, the *SS SOLARWIND* is environmentally friendly. Its aerodynamic shape reduces drag. Its primary propulsion system runs on non-polluting LNG (Liquefied Natural Gas). It also has 10 photovoltaic sails and wind generators that can extend skyward or retract to the deck while in port or when passing under bridges. Its sails are covered with solar panels that automatically move to capture the sun's rays and the wind. When there is no wind, the boat can activate a solar sailing mode. The masts are fitted with a washing system to keep the solar panels clean and working properly.

Much of the power generated by the sails supports the massive hotel and administrative lighting, kitchen, entertainment, heating and a/c needs of the ship but can be used for limited propulsion backup, if necessary, making the vessel a 3-way hybrid – wind, sun and LNG. Waste water is largely recycled or used in the on board gardens. The system results in substantial ecological and budgetary savings.

She has a total pax (passenger) capacity of 1700, fitted out with over 650 luxury suites and a crew size of 1200. An excellent service ratio! We are among the first passengers on her maiden voyage after her successful sea trials and shakedown.

As our story proceeds you'll meet the *SOLARWIND*'s command and crew. *(Listed up front under The Players.)*

We're halfway through our 14 day tour. We left Fort Lauderdale Florida; covered Nassau, Bahamas; St. Thomas, Virgin Islands and San Juan, Puerto Rico; Our next ports of call are Grand Turk Island in the Turks & Caicos; Amber Cove in the Dominican Republic; Grand Cayman; Belize City, Belize; Cozumel, Mexico and then return to Ft Lauderdale.

Thus far on our voyage, we've had an unsettling series of adventures leading up to fighting off a malware attack that threatened to totally cripple the vessel. Octavius' step brother, Agrippa, The Bear Faced Liar and former Casino Manager was an important negative influence in the whole affair. That occasioned the arrival on board of FBI Special Agent Honey Badger, a long time associate of the Octavians. After dealing with the attackers, she decided to take a little R&R and stayed aboard the *SOLARWIND*. Finally, we thought we could catch our collective breaths and enjoy what was left of the cruise *but it was not to be.* Book 18 ended with the Twins discovery of a dead body. Herewith:

The Twins ran off to the Imperial Suite and rushed through the door knocking Carlos the butler, over in the process. "Mom, Dad! Guess what! A body! He's dead! We found him!"

Belinda reacted first. "Who's dead? What happened?"

Arabella caught her breath and sputtered. "We were looking for towel animals for the Scavenger Hunt and we saw this bull floating in the VIP pool. We called security. They're there now."

Before Bel could ask 'who' again, there was a knock on the door. Chief Security Officer Dudley Diomede entered. "Doctor Bear, Bearoness. Sorry to disturb you but we have an incident and I could use your detection skills. We have a dead body at the VIP pool. Your kids discovered it."

McTavish looked shocked. "Are we in trouble? We didn't do anything except call security."

The Albatross shook his head and squawked, "No! No! You're fine." He looked at the Great Bear and Belinda. "It's that obnoxious bovine Texas oil tycoon, Humphrey Vaquero. The guards thought he was drunk as usual and had fallen in. But then one of them noticed stab wounds in his back. This wasn't an accident. He was murdered. His wife's in hysterics and blaming the ship."

Octavius got to his feet, looked at the albatross and said, "Show me! Call Agent Badger. I think we may need the FBI."

As they left, Belinda shook her head. "Tavi, Tavi, Tavi! Oh, dear! Here we go again. Crime seems to follow us around. Are we ever going to be able to just relax and act like retired animals?"

Good question, Bearoness! Don't count on it.

Sorry it took so long to get started with the action but I wanted to give you the lay of the land *(or sea)*. So, let's get on with our story. I guess I'm still glad I signed on for this sea-borne melodrama. But I could be back at the Bear's Lair polishing off a drink or two. Oh, well!

Chapter Two

The bull blowhard is certainly dead,
On the water his carcass is spread.
He was floating face down
In the pool. Did he drown?
Or was he stabbed fiercely instead?

The super-large and luxurious Imperial Suite houses Belinda, Octavius and Carlos, their full time butler. The Twins are in an adjoining apartment. Right now, they were bouncing along with their Dad and the Security Officer to the VIP Pool. They had discovered the bull's body floating in the pool while they were on their scavenger hunt. Humphrey Vaquero, an insufferable Texas oil millionaire, stabbed to death. *(or was he?)*

The security team had pulled the bull's cadaver out of the water and were waiting for the medical crew and the detectives to arrive. Lieutenant Freddi Fox, the Social Directress who was also in charge of the ship's Guest Care Team had the unfortunate duty of informing his wife, Gladys, of the situation. As usual, the heifer was wildly drunk. screamed and tried to attack Freddi. The security officers who had accompanied Lieutenant Fox overwhelmed Gladys and she promptly passed out. It wasn't clear which of the two was more offensive. The wife or her now deceased mate. The Captain, who had arrived at poolside, fully expected Gladys, once she woke up, to be threatening everyone in sight, calling her lawyers to sue the Solar Seas Cruise Ship Company and the *SOLARWIND'S* command and crew for gross negligence, conspiracy and who knows what else. No doubt, she would find several animals to accuse of murder.

The ship's Doctor Goro, a Silverback Gorilla, examined the bull, pronounced him dead and had the medics move the body down to the ship's morgue adjacent to sick bay.

The Guest Care Team, among its many duties, is responsible for handling accidents, deaths and missing parties aboard the ship. The Security Team is in charge of handling crimes. Mostly theft and assaults.

Violent deaths and murders on cruise ships were highly unusual. Even more so on *SOLARWIND* since this was the vessel's maiden voyage. Because she sailed under an American flag, the FBI was the government agency accountable for investigating the event. So much for Agent Badger's vacation.

But international courtesy called for the Captain to report the incident to the local police on Grand Turk, the next port of call, when they arrived. The Turks and Caicos are a British Territory. The Royal Turks and Caicos Islands Police Force has a station at the Grand Turk Cruise Center and a headquarters in Cockburn Town. Staff Captain Montmorency sent a message informing Deputy Commissioner Morris, a feral donkey, of the situation. He agreed to meet the ship at the Cruise Center.

We still had about 200 nautical miles left on our 431 mile transfer from Puerto Rico to Grand Turk. *(That would be followed by a shorter 120 mile hop to Amber Cove in the Dominican Republic.)* Was that enough time for the Great Bear and the shipboard Octavians to assist Agent Badger and Security Officer Diomede in sorting out the blustering bovine's demise? We'd have to see. And, oh yes, let's not forget the Twins who had discovered the body and now decided to make it the centerpiece of their next Internet game - *Bears at Sea*.

A large group assembled in the morgue as Dr. Goro began his examination. Belinda joined the party. Questions and opinions fired back and forth. Motive, means and opportunity – the crime solver's triple play.

Motive? Who would want to see the Houston bull dead? Better to ask who didn't! Humphrey Vaquero did not make friends easily. Pardon the pun but he was a bully. Not that he cared. His vast wealth and dominating attitude toward all and sundry made relationships irrelevant. Or so it seemed.

As far as Means were concerned, the team had not yet examined the wounds in detail but a long knife or other pointed instrument would not be difficult to pick up anywhere and after the deed was done, chucked over the side of the moving vessel.

Opportunity? The bull was in his typical drunken state and could have been easily lured to the VIP deck in his stupor – or stabbed elsewhere and then dumped in the pool. That latter possibility was a bit of a stretch. Humphrey was big, heavy animal, too bulky for one individual to heave over the deck railing and into the sea. The pool was a different matter. Easy to push the dead or dying bull into the water and hold him down if necessary. They'd have to check to see whether he died of his wounds or drowning. The Doctor was making that call right now.

Freddi Fox arrived at the morgue looking disconsolate. She shook her head and said to the Captain and anyone else who was listening. "That heifer is a real piece of work. *(if she is a heifer)* I sympathize with her loss but she's awake and having herself a good case of drink inspired hysterics. She has accused the cruise line of everything from negligence to deliberate murder. She's been on the ship-to-shore phone to her lawyers and having a representative fly into Grand Turk to take up the case."

The Captain nodded and shrugged. "It never rains but it pours. Let's keep this as confidential as we can. We don't want to scare the passengers or start up major scandal sessions. It's a good thing the press are no longer on board. or we'd have a media orgy on our paws. They all exited at San Juan. I've been in contact with Wally Wapiti, our CEO, our Corporate Attorney Emilia Emu and Corporate Security Officer Pablo Puma. They're already up to their ears dealing with the malware perpetrators. *(See Book 18)* They're pleased we have an FBI presence on board."

Freddi continued. "Doctor Bear, you'll be happy to know that you, your twins, the Bearoness, the Captain, the Shearings, the entire casino, security, medical, restaurant and bar staffs, Lieutenant Diomede and I have all been accused by her of killing Humphrey Vaquero. It would be funny if it wasn't so damn serious and irritating."

Doctor Goro took that moment to make his announcement. "He died of drowning. Water in his lungs. The stab wounds were administered post mortem. They are superficial. Looks like someone just wanted to add a little vengeance to the murder. His alcohol level is astounding. Four times the legal limit anywhere. Even for an animal his size, that's a lot of liquor. A few bruises probably incurred by being shoved into the pool and held under. You folks are the detectives but I'm willing to bet more than one individual was involved. Even if he was out of it before he was drowned, he'd be a real pawful for a single killer."

Octavius asked. "Do you think he was drugged, Doctor/"

"Possible. I'm going to do an analysis although that much alcohol alone would have had him pretty woozy."

Special Agent Badger thanked the gorilla, turned to the Social Directress and asked. "I recognize the names she's accusing except for the Shearings. Who are they?"

Captain Lion spoke up. "They're husband and wife sheep. Among the company's very special VIP Old Faithful passengers. They've been sailing on Solar Seas cruises since the firm's origination. We made an extra effort to get them on *SOLARWIND'S* maiden cruise. Lovely couple."

Octavius added. "They are also the Vaquero's financial advisors. Texas Capital in Austin. I heard the bull giving Gideon Shearing a hard time about being on a cruise when he should be making money for him and his wife."

I laughed. "You and the entire dining room. That bovine had only one volume - super-loud."

The FBI agent said, "So Gladys thinks the sheep killed him."

Diomede screeched. "Who knows what she thinks, if anything. She's a hyper agitated drunk. I don't think she's been sober for one moment on this entire cruise. Sozzled or passed out. She's worse than her husband. The bar staff won't serve either of them anymore. So, they've sneaked their own supply of booze on board. Probably from the duty-free shops at our ports of call. When she's conscious, she insults anyone who comes in her path. The staff hate both of them."

The Great Bear looked at the Security Officer. "That remark doesn't help narrow down the list of suspects."

The albatross shrugged. "Sorry. I'm just a dumb ship's cop."

Agent Badger patted him on his wing. "No problem. I guess we better start some interviews. She turned to Freddi and Diomede. Can we get an office, preferably out of the passenger traffic. Let's start with the security team that pulled him out of the pool. Octavius, I want to talk with your twins."

Belinda smiled. "Oh, they'll be thrilled." She thought to herself, "Those kids have the same 'talent' their sire has. If there's a crime or wrongdoing in the vicinity, they'll get involved. It goes all the way back to when they were infant cubs. Like father, like son and daughter. No doubt, they're already plotting out a murder subroutine for their latest Internet game. What's it called? Bears on the Ocean? No, *Bears at Sea!*"

The Development of Civilization Volume 19 Part 2
Security Officers, Detectives and Special Agents

From "An Introduction to Faunapology"

by Octavius Bear Ph.D.

Security Officers and Departments are primarily charged with protective duties and incident response. They may have a variety of specialized roles such as perimeter security, interior and exterior, structural and contents protection, cybersecurity, merchant and bank protection, bodyguard and personal safety, military policing, patrol and watch, screening, access management, demonstration and riot control, protection of personal transport (aircraft, ships, trains, busses) and commercial traffic, infrastructure safety, alarm systems, risk assessment and planning.

A Detective is an investigator, usually a member of a law enforcement agency. They collect information to solve crimes by talking to witnesses and informants, collecting physical evidence, or searching records in databases. This enables them to arrest criminals and get them convicted in court. A detective may work for the police or privately as I and the Octavians do.

A detective (or in the UK, enquiry agent) can be a licensed or unlicensed person who solves offenses, including historical crimes, by examining and evaluating clues and personal records in order to uncover the identity and/or whereabouts of criminals. Some, like us, are private persons, and may be known as private investigators, or shortened to simply "private eyes".

That defines the Octavians. We usually work in close coordination with members of local, national and international law enforcement, worldwide. Some of our major contacts are Chief Inspector Bruce Wallaroo of Interpol and the Australian Federal Police; members of Scotland and Shetland Yard; the French Sureté and Special Agents Fernando Hermano and Honey Badger of the U.S. FBI.

Forensic crime scene investigators document an active crime or accident scene and collect, classify and identify evidence that can later be analyzed in a lab and used in court.

A __Special Agent__ is an __investigator or detective for a governmental or independent agency,__ who serves in criminal investigatory positions. Additionally, in the U.S. many federal and state "Special Agents" operate in "criminal intelligence" based roles as well.

Most people holding the title of "Special Agent" are law enforcement officers under state or federal law (with some also being dual intelligence operatives such as with the FBI). These law enforcement officers are distinctly empowered to conduct both major and minor criminal investigations and have arrest authority.

Additionally, most US Special Agents are authorized to carry firearms both on and off duty due to their status as law enforcement officers. In US federal law enforcement, the title of "Special Agent" is used almost exclusively for federal and military criminal investigators.

Chapter Three

Agent Badger is there on the scene
And she starts her detecting routine
Her vacation's been shot
By a very dead sot.
So she's feeling especially mean.

Belinda was right. The Twins were at it again. Even though they had turned their existing games over to the enthusiastic paws of the gamester geeks at the UUI Hexagon Deep Data Center in Kentucky while they toured the universe, they couldn't resist developing new electronic contests. They had just started design work on their next offering – *Bears at Sea* – built around their recent malware adventures and the wonders of the *SS SOLARWIND*. This current situation *(with a murder no less)* put a whole new spin on things. The two of them had found the body of the obnoxious bull floating in the VIP Pool. Who had killed the unbearable bovine? The Twins had to solve this one! Their players would go wild. Right now, they were due to chat with FBI Special Agent Honey Badger.

The Agent stared at the ceiling and sighed. Her small black eyes were framed by two white chin curves and a stripe running down between them from the top of her head to the tip of her equally black nose. The Social Directress had found her an office on the administrative deck away from the tourist eyes and ears. The ship's security team who had pulled Humphrey's body out of the water had just left They didn't add much to her knowledge. She waited for the Twins to arrive.

A knock on the door! *(Unusual! The two juveniles usually just burst in. Were they maturing?)* Arabella said. "Agent Badger, hello! You wanted to see us?"

The FBI operative smiled *(to the extent a badger can)* and said. "Wow! You two are sprouting. You've grown twice your size since I've seen you last and that was less than a year ago."

McTavish grinned. "Well, you know Mom and Dad are pretty big bears. We take after them."

"Yes, and they're pretty smart bears, too. You inherited their brains as well as their brawn. I hope you don't have your father's temper."

"Nope, we're calm and cool. Well, most of the time. I have to admit finding that dead bull sort of shook us."

"I guess it would. That's what I want to talk to you about. You guys have very sharp memories. Play that episode back for me."

Arabella ran a paw over her face. "We were on the multi-deck scavenger hunt. We were a team of six. Two wolverines, two racoons and us. We drew straws. They had other stuff to dig up. We had to find some towel animals made by the pool deck cleaning crews. We decided this late in the evening all the towels on the Lido deck would have been used. So we went to the VIP pool where nobody was around. We found a couple of terry cloth giraffes. We had our prizes. We were about to return to the starting point when I noticed a large figure floating face down in the otherwise empty pool. I shouted, "Who is that? Tavi, Help! Get security!"

McTavish picked up the story. "Arabella stayed there. I ran and got a couple of the guards who were patrolling the VIP deck. They saw the body floating in the pool and jumped in and pulled him out. It took both of them. That bull is heavy. We thought he had passed out. We've seen him and his wife dead drunk *(sorry)* a couple of times. The guards called the Security Officer and he called the Captain. That's when we ran back to the suite to tell Mom and Dad. We didn't realize he was dead and had been stabbed until we went back with Dad to the pool."

"Did you see or hear anyone while you were gathering your scavenger prizes?"

"Nope. The whole pool area was empty. The other members of our scavenger team were off in other parts of the ship."

The Badger shook her head. "Normally, I'd be able to call in a crime scene investigation group to go over the entire area but we don't have any of those on this ship. The VIP Pool is closed and cordoned off. I'll have to enlist some of the ship's security staff and maybe some of your Dad's Octavians."

Arabella smiled. "Oh, you have a bunch of super crime scene investigators. The Ursulas, Uncle Otto, the Wolves, Chita, Howard, Lord David. They'll find things no other animal would. With a few clues, I'll bet they can reconstruct the whole event. Call Dad!"

"Good idea, kids. I keep forgetting what a great bunch Octavius has with him."

*****

Back in the Imperial Suite, the Great Bear had gathered the Octavians and brought them up to date on the murder in the VIP Pool. The Twins and Agent Badger were in attendance. The ship's security team was not.

"As I understand it, you want help in reconstructing the crime, Agent Badger."

"Yes! Knowing all the tricks your group has up your collective sleeves *(if you are wearing any)* I believe we can gather enough evidence to give us a good fix on who the culprits are."

The Frau's ears twitched, "Culprits? Plural"

"I think so. Very few individual animals on this ship could have dragged that huge bovine into the pool and drowned him by themselves. I also suspect the knife wounds were added after the fact. No proof, but the doctor claims they were not the cause of death."

Octavius remarked, "Gladys Vaquero seems to think, if she thinks at all, that half the ship's population, including present company was responsible for Humphrey's death. Belinda and I are big enough."

Chita laughed. "A nine foot Kodiak topping off an unbearable bull. Sorry, I couldn't resist. By the way, is Gladys Vaquero still a childless heifer? I doubt it. I think she's an over the hill cow. Lost most of her looks. Maybe that's why she drinks although Humphrey wasn't behind the lines in liquor consumption. Between the two of them, they could have won the *SS SOLARWIND* Nastiest Couple and Sots of the Year awards three times over. You know, I wouldn't put it past her to have knocked her husband off. They seemed to hate each other in spite of her hysterics over his death. I think she's an accomplished actress. Of course, she would have needed help but in addition to sloshing in alcohol, she's rolling in dough. Are there hired killers on this ship? What do the spirits say, Giselle?"

The Bichon grinned. "They say you have a very suspicious nature, Madame Catt. But you may be right. Ursulas, can you hack the ship's security camera tapes and track back Humphrey's final moments?"

"We're already on it. We'll build a Virtual Reality scenario and see what comes out of it. Howard, Arabella, McTavish. We could use your help. Your experience in managing systems and constructing games will come in handy. We can use the headsets and specialty computers in the VR room. . Madame Giselle and Otto, you have the AR contact lenses you use in your act. We might want to use them too in tracking down the actors."

Otto, who had been uncharacteristically quiet, held up a box with the lenses and earbuds they used. "Got them here. We need them tonight for our show along with one of the Ursulas." Madame Giselle agreed.

Ursula 16 continued. "Speaking of games, it seems our victim was engaged earlier in a high stakes poker competition in the casino. Unusual. Most of the games are penny-ante to satisfy the tourist newbies. This game was serious. The casino supplied the dealer, seats, cards and table. For some reason, they allowed the chip purchases to exceed the house limits."

The Colonel spoke up. "I believe they would if all the players agreed to higher stakes. The house collects a piece of the game's value in a rake since it's not actually part of the action. Let's see if you can reconstruct the game."

Lord David asked, "Octavius, since your stepbrother Agrippa is on his way to jail for fraud, who is managing the casino? *(See Book 18 -The Bear Faced Liar.)*

"One of the assistant managers has taken over for the duration of the cruise. A female. Laura Llama. Don't know a thing about her. Chita! How would you like to do a little intelligence gathering?"

"One of my specialties. I'll check out the roulette wheels and baccarat tables while I'm at it."

Belinda turned to the Twins. "You two stay out of the casino. You look older than you are and they might let you in. I don't want to hear you're gambling. Even on the slot machines."

Arabella broke out a bearish pout. McTavish said nothing.

Octavius looked at the Special Agent. "I suppose we should let Diomede, Freddi and the Captain in on what we're doing. The participation of the Ursulas will be suitably edited out. I'll take care of that. Want to join me, Agent Badger? Meanwhile, kids, Ursulas, let's see how much Metaverse Magic you can conjure up. Bel, do you feel up to approaching Gladys Vaquero? Bring Freddi with you as part of the Guest Care Team. If the cow is sober enough, maybe you can get some sense out of her."

Chita laughed, "Or maybe you could drown her, too."

The Bearoness shrugged and gave Octavius a look that said. 'we'll talk about this later.'

The group broke up, each to their given assignments. Meanwhile, off the coast of Africa, a few storm clouds were stirring as the *SS SOLARWIND* drew closer to the Turks and Caicos Islands.

The Development of Civilization Volume 19 Part 3
Metaverse, Virtual and Augmented Reality
From "An Introduction to Faunapology"

by Octavius Bear Ph.D.

The Octavians and I have dedicated ourselves to the exploration of the Multiverse. *The multiverse is the totality of the universes that comprise everything that exists in actuality: the entirety of space, time, matter, energy, information, life and the physical laws and constants that govern and describe them. We refer to the different worlds within the multiverse as parallel or alternate universes. The* Multiverse *should not be confused with the* Metaverse *which at this moment has its origins in our own virtual space but may extend far beyond. They both deal with alternate universes. In the Multiverse, they are real. In the Metaverse, they are virtual.*

The Metaverse has been characterized as a version of the Internet that is a single, universal and immersive virtual world facilitated by the use of virtual reality (VR) and augmented reality (AR) devices, infrastructure and software. In colloquial terms, a metaverse is a network of 3D virtual worlds focused on social connections. It may replicate real locations from our own world or create imaginary virtual spaces. Originally created for gamers such as our Twins, these virtual spaces are expanding to be the environment for broader future experiences.

An important distinction: Virtual reality environments totally replace *the outside world. Augmented reality* adds *additional elements to existing space without eliminating perception of our surroundings. Virtual reality devices provide immersion and substitution. Augmented reality supplements but does not displace our physical experiences.*

At the moment, virtual reality (VR) relies on headsets or similar equipment that completely surround the participant's senses to the exclusion of the actual world in which he or she exists. You are literally transported to another environment. Visually and aurally, you're taken to wherever the headset wants you to go—the outside world is replaced with a virtual one. Touch and smell are under development. VR also allows you to personally inject yourself in a variety of modes and forms. Avatars, representative images that represent the participants, have been used extensively in on-line games. Now it's in use in other arenas including complete civilizations.

Augmented reality (AR) can be implemented in a variety of ways ranging from simple images or sounds added to one's vision and hearing to multiple, dynamic, simultaneous sources of information. This is all while still remaining conscious of one's actual surroundings. Heads-up flight or battlefield management systems are classic examples. Smart glasses are frequently used matched with headphones or earbuds. (See Book 17 The Octavian Cases.) AR displays can offer something as simple as a data overlay that shows the time to something as complicated as holograms floating in the middle of a room. The two metaverse technologies (AR & VR) differ from each other and have different applications. But they both extend our abilities, perceptions and experiences in ways yet to be fully explored, explained or exploited.

Shortly, you'll find we make use of VR to track down a killer.

Chapter Four

The Octavians take up the case
And they start off by trying to trace
The bull's movements that night,
Was he killed in a fight?
He was bruised on his legs and his face.

The investigation proceeds!

At the Captain's direction and much to the tourists' annoyance, the Social Directress closed the Virtual Reality Hall to passengers. She claimed system maintenance! The Twins, Howard and two Ursulas activated the ship's Virtual Reality environment and made contact with the VR/AR teams back at the Kentucky Hexagon. They proceeded to sweep up the ship's security tapes from all over the vessel. They created an avatar for Humphrey Vaquero and began tracking him for the previous 24 hours. Bearyl and Bearnice helped with the acting as other players appeared and established relations with the bull.

Chita, Ben, Gal and the Colonel headed off to the casino to interview Laura Llama and investigate the high stakes poker game Humphrey had been engaged in.

Belinda met Freddi Fox and much to their mutual distaste sought out the 'distraught' widow.

The Frau, Otto and Dancing Dan went back to the morgue and joined the Doctor and Chief Security Officer in further examining the corpse.

Madame Giselle, Jaguar Jack and Lord David went to the VIP deck where a pair of security officers were emptying the pool and looking for evidence.

The rest of the ship's command group went about the business of sailing and managing the *SS SOLARWIND,* keeping an eye out for Grand Turk and some iffy weather rising across the Atlantic off the coast of Africa.

*****

41

On the bridge: Octavius joined the Captain, Staff Captain, First Officer and Chief Purser in the Captain's Conference room. Captain Lion and the Great Bear discussed the situation generally. Octavius then outlined how the Octavians, the Social Directress, Doctor, Security Chief and Special Agent Badger were set up as crime scene investigators and how they were going about their specific tasks.

The Chief Purser had been acting as the Captain's liaison with the Solar Seas corporate office. In addition to being concerned with how long they could keep the story from reaching the passengers, Corporate was eager to see the crime solved and the upcoming visit from the Vaquero's lawyer or lawyers brought under control. All this was on top of managing the malware attack situation in Tampa. Special Agent Fernando Hermano had flown up from the San Juan Field Office to lead the FBI's participation in that can of worms.

As far as the murder went, Agent Badger was charged with supervising the shipboard activities and dealing with the Grand Turk's Police representative when the ship arrived at the islands.

*****

The Vaquero's Suite on the Empire Deck: Chief Purser Gillian Greyhound had decided to join Belinda and Social Directress Freddi Fox in dealing with Gladys Vaquero. They felt an all-female team would have a better chance of calming the alcohol soaked heifer down. Perhaps the presence of the aristocratic Bearoness would have a cowing effect (no pun) on the snobby bovine. Let's see.

They knocked on the suite door and were greeted by a nurse from the ship's medical staff. She saluted the Chief Purser and walked out into the passageway to greet them. "This one is a real case. I've dealt with alcoholic withdrawal symptoms before but I'm surprised she's still alive. Of course, the loss of her mate in a such a horrible fashion is enough to set anyone off."

The Purser asked. "Can we see her?

"I guess so but I can't guarantee her reaction. She's out for everybody's pelt, including mine. She was a swift pain in the rear before but this has pushed her over the edge. We don't have a psychiatrist on board but maybe we can get her some help at Grand Turk."

Freddi agreed to check if a 'shrink' would be available at the Grand Turk Cruise Center.

The nurse opened the suite door and called out. "Mrs. Vaquero, there several ladies here to see you."

"Tell them to go away and you go away. I want my lawyer as soon as we dock. I'm going to sink this ship and the entire cruise line. Oooh! Humphrey!"

Not quite as opulent as Belinda's Imperial Suite but sumptuous enough, the rooms were a mess. Gladys had taken out her drunken wrath on the maid and nurse and had tossed bedding, vases, glasses and furniture upside down and scattered throughout. The nurse had ensured there were no liquor bottles available which had only served to enrage the cow further. As the trio advanced into the room she screamed at the two uniformed officers and then seeing Belinda for the first time, stopped in mid-rant.

Taken aback by the bejeweled polar sow who was as large as she was and clearly a member of global aristocracy, the cow's snobbery kicked in. "Ms. Bear, who are you and why are you here with these two officious phonies of the ship's staff?"

Frowning, Belinda poured it on. "I'm Bearoness Belinda Béarnaise Bruin Bear *(nee Black)*. My husband is Doctor Octavius Bear PhD, sole owner of UUI Industries and a world-famous detective. We met the other night but I doubt you remember. We two and our team of highly skilled crime fighting experts, the Octavians, are engaged in seeking out your husband's killer or killers. I assume you want justice done and will be willing to answer a few questions."

The rapidly sobering cow looked around the room wildly, gulped, shook her head to clear her muzzy brain and said, "All right. But get those two out of here and this stupid nurse, too."

43

"Sorry. These officers are in charge of the ship's Guest Care Team and responsible for monitoring and managing these kind of terrible events. They have to stay."

Gladys was ready to unleash another rant and refuse to speak without her lawyer but thought better of it. Her social snobbery took over. This polar sow was impressive. A member of the nobility! Someone she probably didn't want to cross. She could always refuse the individual questions.

"All right but I don't know anything of use."

Belinda smiled *(not reassuringly with her array of teeth)*. "Let us decide that. First, can you track back from dinner last night until the last time you saw your husband alive?"

"Humphrey left me in the dining room. He was on his way to a high stakes poker game in the casino."

"Who with?"

"I don't know. There was lot of money involved and the casino had set up a special table for the players."

"How many players?"

"Don't know that either. Humphrey went off and I returned to our suite. I fell asleep and didn't wake up until these idiots came and told me my mate was dead." Another round of hysterics. The nurse went to assist her but was shaken off. "Get away from me, you witch. You probably want to kill me, too."

Belinda looked puzzled. "Why would she want to do that?"

The cow screamed, "Captain's orders! He knows I'm going to sue him, his crew, this ship and that crummy cruise company for every dollar they have and then some. I'm going to bankrupt and destroy them for good. I'll sell this stupid ship for scrap. They need to get rid of me like they did Humphrey. I want my lawyers and I want protection. Bearoness, if your husband is a big shot detective, get him and his flunkies down here to keep me safe."

The greyhound Chief Purser had remained silent during this tirade but broke in before Belinda could answer. "We have an FBI Special Agent on board and she is in charge of the investigation. She'll be down to see you momentarily and see to your safety. As I understand it, your lawyers are flying into Grand Turk and will meet the ship when it arrives."

"They better or that law firm will be dead meat. Everybody out. I want to sleep. Oooh Humphrey!"

The nurse took up a chair in the suite's lounge. Out in the passageway, the Purser turned to Belinda. "Thank you Bearoness. Hurricane Gladys is a real piece of work, isn't she? Speaking of hurricanes, there's a storm brewing off the African coast. Not sure of its speed, nature or direction but we'll be in and out of Grand Turk before it arrives, if it does arrive. I'd rather be tied up in Amber Cove in the Dominican Republic if we have to ride out some weather."

Belinda winced. 'We went through a hefty monsoon storm when we were out on the Great Barrier Reef in Australia. Not much fun. Of course we were on a relatively small superyacht not a large aerodynamic vessel like the *SS SOLARWIND*. I suppose you'd all like to find out how she stands up to Mother Nature's nastiness."

Freddi Fox yipped. "This heifer is more than enough nastiness for me, thank you. I'll get Agent Badger down here to take her on. From what I've seen and heard, she won't take any nonsense from our alcoholic friend."

Belinda chuckled. "No, I've spent a fair amount of time with Honey Badger. She has a low tolerance for fools. Let's go see her."

*****

In the ship's casino: Business was slow. The ringing bells, clatter and annoying "boop-boop" music of the slot machines interrupted by the occasional laughs, barks, moos, yips, grunts or growls of the few players there provided all the background noise there was. The ambient lights were low except for the flashing one-arm bandits. *(Actually that phrase no longer applied since the slots were all electronic and push button controlled.)*

Chita, Ben, Gal, a ship Security Officer and the Colonel strolled in looking for Laura Llama, the acting casino manager. Octavius' step Brother Agrippa had briefly held that job but was arrested for using fraudulent credentials and abetting the malware attack on the ship. He was cooling his paws in the FBI's Tampa facility awaiting arraignment.

Laura Llama had been an assistant casino manager on several of the Solar Seas Cruise Ship Company's vessels and was now trying to prove her ability to manage the *SS SOLARWIND's* games full time.

The tall, tan, graceful lamoid was wearing an officer's cap, a black bolero style jacket with gold epaulettes and a gold bow tie around her slender neck. She was talking to the croupier at the inactive roulette table when the quintet came over. She turned her attention to the group. The Lama Glama *(scientific name)* are intelligent, highly sociable and good natured. Laura was no exception, She flicked the long lashes of her deep grey eyes and said. "Hello Folks! Looking for a little action? Probably not with one of our security officers in tow. I'm Lieutenant Laura Llama. I'm the manager here. How can I help you?"

Chita responded, "Sorry, Ms. Llama. Not a gambler in the group. We're private detectives acting for the FBI and Ship Security in the murder of Humphrey Vaquero. He was found dead floating in the VIP swimming pool. Are you familiar with the event?"

The llama nodded. "I've been informed by the bridge. I've been expecting someone to come by.

The security officer, a large mastiff, said. "I'm Ensign Farley. We have some questions we'd like to ask you. By the way, we have the Captain's permission, if you'd like to check."

The llama looked at each member of the quintet and said, "Not necessary! Let's go back to my office. Sounds like we need some privacy."

Two white tigers, one cheetah and a wolf *(plus one mastiff)*. Fearsome predators in the wild but Laura showed no sign of concern. Chita introduced the Octavians and said. "We understand Humphrey Vaquero was engaged in a high stakes, private poker tournament here last night. Can you fill us in on the game and the other players?"

"Sure! The ship's casino is happy to supply table space, cards, chips, dealer services and refreshments to any respectable parties who request it. In exchange, we take a modest rake from the game's pot since we are not actually involved in the game except to supply a dealer. Some groups even deal themselves but we keep a watch on the play to avoid any conflicts."

Ben asked, "You say 'respectable parties.' Please explain."

'Oh, we get the occasional drunks or rabble rousers flashing wads of money and insisting we let them 'get a game together.' We know how to handle them. Very rarely, we have to bring in the security team." She nodded at Ensign Farley.

Gal looked at her brother and then asked. "Were the animals who were playing with Mr. Vaquero 'respectable'?"

"It started out that way. There were six of them. Tough looking customers but not unusual for poker players. A little loud, especially the bull. Unfortunately, the game broke up with accusations of cheating. Our dealer had to shut the game down and called me over. Mr. Vaquero had been taking full advantage of our drinks service and so were a couple of his competitors. He was drunk. They were playing Texas Hold'em with table stakes. The pots were getting pretty pricey. He was losing big time. That's when he started yelling about being cheated."

"His partners tried to calm him down but he is (or was) a big animal and wasn't taking too kindly to being shut up, losing his money and not having a chance to win it back. He was struggling but they finally managed to get him out of the casino. I was about to call security but the players said they didn't want an incident and would take care of it."

"Who were the other players?"

"I thought you'd ask me that. Here's the list. Every one of them from luxury class. Besides Vaquero, there were two other bulls – the Wind Brothers, Charley and Wilbur. A wolverine by the name of Sydney. I think he's a professional. A female cougar, would you believe. Tough looking dolly. Carlotta Corona." *(She cast a sideways glance at Chita and Gal.)* And oh, yes, a sheep called Gideon Shearing. How's that for a name?"

The Colonel looked at Chita and winked. They said nothing. "Who was the dealer?"

"One of our old timers. Luke. He's a llama, too and before you ask, our relationship is purely professional."

The group laughed.

"Oh, one more thing. Once we ended the game, after taking our rake, we divided the pot up evenly among the players, including Vaquero. Nobody was particularly happy about that but it's a casino rule if play is stopped."

Ensign Farley thanked her, took the list, looked around and asked. "Is Luke here?"

"No, his shift starts in a couple of hours but by then we may be in Grand Turk and we'll have to shut down. He should be in his cabin."

The group left. Chita took a shot at a slot machine on the way out and lost a dollar.

*****

At the VIP Pool: Madame Giselle, Jaguar Jack and Lord David approached the VIP deck where a pair of security officers and a couple of deck hands were draining the pool and looking for evidence.

"It's amazing the things you find when you drain a pool." One of the security crew said to the trio. "We find some of the damndest stuff at the bottom of the Lido Pool, too. Of course, that one is huge and has a lot more bathers but this one has quite a collection. Towels, all kinds of lotion, toys, parts of bathing suits, glasses, hearing aids, who knows what else."

One of the deck hands shouted up from the now empty bottom. "I think we found something. Looks like a wallet. Soaked, of course. What was the victim's name."

"Humphrey Vaquero!"

"Yeah, this is his. Money, credit cards, driver's license and some strange looking pieces of paper. One of them looks like an IOU for several thousand dollars. There are several, Barely readable. The names and dates are mostly blotted out. Here!"

He tossed it up to the security officer who in turn showed it around to the Bichon, Dalmatian and Jaguar. Jack whistled *(or as close to a whistle as a jaguar can get.)* "Looks like somebody or somebodies were into our friend for quite a pile."

Giselle barked, "Well, if we were looking for motive, that might be it. Let's get together with Octavius and the FBI Special Agent."

*****

At the Morgue: The Frau, Otto and Dancing Dan were with the Doctor and Chief Security Officer further examining the corpse:

Doctor Goro finished up his post mortem assessment, laid down his tools and turned to the group who were standing by. "As I said, definitely drowning. Bruises on his legs and face. He may have fallen. He was drunk, after all. The stab wounds were made after his death. They seem almost to be random. I can't put any rhyme or reason to them. Have they found the weapon?"

Chief Security Officer Diomede squawked. "Yes, We think so! We found a knife under a chair near the pool. We originally thought the weapon, whatever it was, had long since settled to the bottom of the ocean. But this may be it. Can you describe the wounds?"

"Short sharp blade. Like a steak knife or a Swiss Army knife. Pretty common."

"That's what we found. We're testing it right now.

The Frau snorted. "Curiouser and Curiouser. Thank you, Herr Doctor. Do you have any questions, Otto or Herr Dan? If not, let's go back to Doctor Bear and the Special Agent."

Negative nods from both. They thanked the doctor and left the room.

Chapter Five

The bull bully got very upset.
He was losing on each poker bet.
If his luck didn't break
He would drop his whole stake.
He could certainly end up in debt.

In the ship's Virtual Reality Hall. The Twins, Howard, the two Ursulas and I activated the V/R environment and made contact with the Metaverse teams back at the Hexagon for support. They proceeded to load up the ship's security tapes from all over the vessel. They created an avatar for Humphrey Vaquero and began tracking him for the previous 24 hours. Bearyl and Bearnice helped with the acting as other players appeared and interacted with the bull. Unfortunately they had no sound but Bearyl was skilled at animal lip reading and was reproducing some of the conversations. They picked him up with his wife in the dining room. They seemed to be arguing *(What else was new?)* and when he left her they followed him out to the casino, filling in some of the dead spots where the security cameras were not active or unavailable.

Vaquero had clearly over imbibed and was unsteady on his legs. He joined the other five members of the poker party in the casino as well as Luke, the dealer. Laura Llama made a brief appearance at the table. She seemed to be explaining the rules of a private shipboard poker game. Humphrey seemed most impatient and loquacious and was urging the dealer to get the game started.

The action proceeded fast and furious for about an hour. The wolverine and Gideon Shearing were folding quite often. The female cougar seemed to be having a winning streak. The other bulls, Charley and Wilbur were winning and losing sporadically but Humphrey was not doing well at all. Finally he exploded. Tossed his cards on the table, took a swat at the dealer and missed. He shouted at the cougar who maintained her cool and stared back. The wolverine and sheep tried to calm him down and the Wind Brothers joined in. Laura Llama came over to the table. She looked at

Luke, the dealer and with a swipe of her hoof across her neck, shut the game down.

Another round of tape downloading was kicked off.

*****

The *SS SOLARWIND* was approaching Grand Turk and the Cruise Center where she was scheduled to tie up and allow the day trippers to debark. The beach was directly adjacent to the slips along with bars, restaurants, shops and the police center.

The Captain and FBI Special Agent, as a courtesy, agreed to report the incident to the local police on Grand Turk when they arrived. The Turks and Caicos are a British Territory. The Royal Turks and Caicos Islands Police Force has a station at the Grand Turk Cruise Center. Staff Captain Montmorency sent a message informing Deputy Commissioner Morris, a feral donkey, of the situation. He agreed to meet the ship. His car pulled up to the slip and he watched the sleek vessel maneuver up to the dock. He stared at the long aerodynamic shape and the wind/solar sails pointing up to the skies. He turned to the constable in the driver's seat and said. "Well, this is a new one on me. Not sure what I'm lookin' at, Bradley. It's obviously a ship. It just came sailing in here but it's like nothing I've ever seen before. What are those things that look like extended fins?"

The constable replied. "They're solar panels and wind sails, sir. They help power the ship. There are ten of them and they're retractable. There was a description in today's press and on the Internet."

"Wind sails, eh? Back to the future." The donkey brayed.

As soon as the ship was secured, the uniformed Deputy Commissioner got out of his car, trotted over and flashed his warrant card at the ship's security officer managing the gangway and asked to be directed to the Captain and FBI Special Agent. Staff Captain Montmorency was watching from the top of the stairs and came down to greet the policeman. "Welcome aboard, Commissioner. Sorry to be bringing a murdered body onto your patch but I believe we have everything in hand. As I told you, Special Agent Badger from the FBI

51

has taken charge. Since we're flying an American flag, she has jurisdiction but I'm sure she will be eager to bring you up to speed."

"Thank you, Captain. Lead on!"

*****

Also waiting on the causeway at the Cruise Center were two lawyers from the firm of Marshall and Lore, summoned by Gladys Vaquero. They had flown in from Houston on a Vaquero Oil private jet to THE GRAND TURK JAMES ALEXANDER GEORGE SMITH McCARTNEY INTERNATIONAL AIRPORT, the only airport on the island. *(Its name is longer than its runway.)* The two attorneys had taken a cab to the Cruise center and had arrived just as the ship was docking.

They were not looking forward to this meeting. They had many prior experiences with both Vaqueros and they had not been pleasant. The wife was a special trial. *(pun intended)* and now the bull was dead – murdered if Gladys was to be believed. They hoped she was sober. The senior partner, Maximillian Marshall, a ferret, supervised all aspects of the high value Vaquero account. The litigious bovines always had a string of lawsuits in progress. With any luck, the lawyers might be able to transport Humphrey Vaquero's dead body and Gladys Vaquero's live (?) carcass back to Houston on the jet. They wanted to get both of them off the ship ASAP and keep Gladys from making a terrible situation totally intolerable as she probably would. Probably a vain hope, however.

Criminal law was not Max's specialty. Especially shipboard murder. For that, he had brought along the firm's expert on cruising and aviation crime, Esther Eagle. She and Special Agent Badger knew each other. The relationship was borderline cordial. The Solar Seas Corporate Attorney Emilia Emu who was in Tampa on the malware case, had arranged for a Zoom hookup with all of the parties involved. They spoke to the security officer manning the gangplank. He called up to the bridge and was instructed to admit them. Let the games begin!

First stop: the FBI. Octavius, Captain Lion, the Purser and Diomede, the ship's security officer were together with Agent Badger in the office the social directress had set aside for her use. The Solar Seas

52

attorney was tied in on a Zoom link and appeared on a large TV screen. The Grand Turk Deputy Commissioner had just wound up his discussion with them and offered any assistance the island police could provide. No passengers were staying over on Grand Turk so ship's security could determine that all parties had returned from their day trip at the end of the day. If anyone failed to show up, the local police would start an immediate search. He was thanked profusely for his help. He left just in time for the lawyers to arrive.

The Special Agent greeted them and braced for an attack. Surprisingly, the ferret and eagle, were suave and gracious. A welcome relief from their client's rants and raves. Introductions all around. Octavius with his nine foot height and significant girth was a bit off putting. So was the leonine Captain. Max Marshall opened the discussion.

"Lady and gentlebeasts. Marshall and Lore has been the exclusive law firm for Vaquero Oil and the personal attorneys for Mr. and Mrs. Vaquero for over ten years. During that time, we have represented all parties in a wide variety of commercial and personal litigation including, I am unhappy to say, several criminal cases. Mr. Vaquero was troublesome but a skilled businessman. *("When he was sober," Octavius thought.)* Mrs. Vaquero keeps up a steady stream of personal lawsuits, many of which we have won for her. *("That cow could start a fight in an empty room")*

The Emu interrupted from the Zoom screen. "We have heard her threats, counsellor, and our corporate office regards them as being without merit. Your firm's income will no doubt benefit from her vindictiveness but I believe she will have wasted all of our time, expense and efforts if any of her bullying gets to the courts."

The Eagle responded, "We are not ambulance chasers, Ms. Emu. Our corporate accounts provide us with very significant revenue and we are not interested in pursuing frivolous claims. However, a client of ours has been murdered on your ship and we expect to see major due diligence being exerted by Solar Seas, the staff of this vessel and of course, the FBI. We will hold off on any legal proceedings in spite of Mrs. Vaquero's insistence until we are convinced either justice has been well served or there are legitimate grounds for litigation."

The Special Agent growled. "Fair enough, Ms. Eagle and Mr. Marshall. You should know that I have called on Dr. Octavius Bear here and his team of formidable detectives to assist me and the ship's security staff. They are already engaged in reconstructing the crime scene and events leading up to Humphrey Vaquero's demise."

"We are familiar with Dr. Bear's and his staff's reputation and are pleased they are involved. We look forward to a speedy resolution to this unhappy event. No, we have another issue to discuss. We arrived here on a Vaquero corporate jet of sufficient size and range to take us back to Houston. We wish to transport Mr. Vaquero's body and Mrs. Vaquero with us on our return trip."

Honey Badger looked at Octavius and the Captain. "What say you, gentlebeasts?"

The Captain was eager to get the cadaver and troublesome 'heifer' off his ship. Octavius, being suspicious of her, was of two minds, but agreed, provided the law firm kept her under surveillance back in Houston. He said nothing about their Virtual Reality process reproducing the events leading up to the bull's demise. The technical team was still sorting through the ship-wide security tapes and creating VR scenarios.

The Captain saw Octavius nod and the Special Agent, Security Officer and Corporate Attorney all agreed. Captain Lion said, "I'll have the Doctor prepare the body for travel. Now, Mr. Marshall and Ms. Eagle, it is up to you to persuade your client to leave the ship and return with you to Houston." The Purser added, "Tell her we will refund all their costs and expenses incurred thus far. That's one lawsuit we can avoid."

The lawyers smiled, shook their heads and said. "Thank you. Will one of you take us to her cabin. We might as well get this over with." The security officer reluctantly volunteered and they got up to leave.

The Purser said, "Please have complimentary dinner and drinks in any of our restaurants before you see her or before you debark. Hardly a bribe on our part. It will take a bit of time for the Doctor to prepare the body and you may want to fortify yourselves before you meet her."

They left. The Emu signed off on Zoom. The Captain returned to the bridge and the Purser had a long list of duties to perform before they left port that evening on their way to Amber Cove.

The Special Agent blew out her cheeks. "That was less painful than I thought it would be. They were actually reasonable. Their client is not. I don't envy them." She turned to Octavius. "They found his wallet in the pool. Usual contents. But it seems he had a number of big ticket IOU's. We couldn't identify who the debtors were. The water had smeared the ink or the signatures were unintelligible. How are your technical wizards doing with the virtual reality?"

"That's what I intend to find out. I'll keep you posted. Do you want us to examine the wallet and IOU's?"

"Yes please. I have it here." She gave him a plastic specimen bag.

"I'll ask the Frau and Colonel to do a little analysis. Maybe we can figure out a name or two and we have the tapes of whomever he was playing with. The casino manager may help."

The Badger asked, "You think someone wanted to get out of paying up?"

"There have been weaker reasons for murder."

"His wife bothers me."

"She bothers everyone."

"No, I think she's acting. The grief and hysterics are overdone. She's an offensive pain but she's not a full-time drunk. I think she's trying to extort large sums from the cruise company."

"Belinda agrees with you. Female intuition?"

She laughed, "No, female intelligence."

Chapter Six

As the team gets a look at the tape,
The solution begins to take shape.
Humphrey first staggers back
Then they see an attack.
But who killed him and made their escape?

The Virtual Reality exercise was back in action after the newer security tapes had been sorted and processed by the deep data specialists back at the Hexagon. They resumed with Humphrey Vaquero apparently shouting and yelling at all and sundry as he was hustled out of the casino by his poker partners and a ship security officer. Since there was no audio, Bearyl lip read some of the less objectionable curses and threats. Staggering drunkenly, he crashed into a slot machine and bounced off the casino doors. Laura Llama came over to the entrance.

The security officer, wolverine and Gideon Shearing led him to the elevator. The car was too small to accommodate three large bulls especially one who was thrashing around so Wilbur and Charley stayed out in the passageway. The female cougar had remained in the casino and rose to cash in her chips. Just before the elevator door closed, the wolverine dodged back out and joined the bulls, leaving the security officer and the sheep to deal with Vaquero.

There was a pause in the action as the team pulled up the elevator's security tape. Humphrey was bouncing back and forth against the walls of the car and almost squashed Gideon Shearing several times. They reached the Empire Deck and the doors opened. More adjustments to pick the trio back up as they lurched out onto the deck toward the stern and the suites surrounding the VIP pool. One of those suites belonged to the Vaqueros. *(Ironically, Special Agent Badger's rooms were right next to theirs. She was down having a late dinner and unaware of what was happening.)* The sheep stepped back and returned to the elevator leaving Humphrey with the security guard. The bull pounded on the suite door and Gladys opened it. The two of them engaged in a vociferous shouting match. Bearyl picked up some of the insults being tossed about. Finally, Humphrey pushed past her and entered the suite, slamming the door in the security officer's face. No further action recorded.

McTavish looked at Howard. "Is that it? How did he end up in the pool?"

Before the porcupine could answer, one of the Ursulas intervened. "Hold on. There's more. Let's just wait out the tapes."

*****

The lawyers, not intent on delaying the inevitable, had passed up the Purser's offer of dinner and drinks and went to face down Gladys Vaquero. They had ordered up a large pickup truck to transport the heifer and her husband's body to the jet waiting at the airport to wing them back to Houston. While Gladys was unconscious, the nurse and maid had packed up his and her clothes and belongings and had the bags and trunk standing by the door to the suite.

She woke up, screaming. She recognized the ferret and said, "It took you long enough to get here. I want to bankrupt this rotten cruise company. I want you to sue them into oblivion."

Max Marshall, who was used to Gladys' uncontrollable rants looked at the Eagle and nodded his head. She nodded back. The nurse and maid were standing on the far side of the lounge entranceway near the stack of luggage.

"We'll see to it, Mrs. Vaquero but first we need to get you and Humphrey's body off this ship. We have a plane ready at the airport waiting to take us back to Houston. Your bags are all packed. The FBI agent has agreed to release his body and we know you want to accompany it back home. By the way, I'm Esther Eagle, a specialist in travel-related criminal law."

"I want justice for Humphrey."

The Eagle stared as only an aquila can. "You'll get it. Don't worry! But first let's debark and go to the plane. You're free to leave. The ship's Purser has eliminated all your charges.'

The heifer snorted. "As well they should. This trip has been a total disaster. All right. Let's go!"

She rose unsteadily to her feet. The nurse came over to assist her. Two crew members were waiting outside the suite to take the baggage down to the waiting pickup. The Purser was standing by the elevator and the social directress was down at the gangway with the security officer to see her into the truck.

The pickup was loaded with the body and luggage. The lawyers and their client got in the cab and the driver headed off to the airport. Esther Eagle had called ahead alerting the pilots and cabin crew to prepare for a quick departure.

With bowls of champagne in their paws, Belinda and Chita watched the procession, unseen on an upper deck. The Bearoness shrugged. "This is only the beginning but at least she and her husband's body are off the ship. I can feel the pressure dropping."

The cat grimaced. "The Solar Seas Company's problems are just starting but those lawyers seem to be rational. Although I doubt they will be able to control her. We have to discover who killed him and why. I wonder how our VR techies are doing."

*****

In the Virtual Reality room, the team had pawsed to further organize the ship's security tapes with special attention to the VIP pool and the Empire Deck. To conserve storage, the cameras usually went quiet after several minutes of inaction although electronic clocks kept track of the passage of time. Any movement would reactivate them. There were no live cameras inside the Vaquero suite. The Hexagon specialists back in Kentucky were working their magic converting the recordings into VR images. They had developed avatars for Humphrey, his poker companions, the Casino manager, security officer and now Gladys. Bearyl had been applying her lip reading skills to the process.

The cameras were mostly dormant as the clocks ticked off the minutes. One couple left their suite on the way to the elevators. Then nothing.

Suddenly, a flash of light as the door to the Vaquero suite opened and Humphrey staggered out with Gladys in hot pursuit. She was swinging a large knife. *(Where did she get that?)* He lurched forward drunkenly and fell face down into the VIP pool. She ran up to him as he was flailing about in the water. BUT instead of trying to help him out, she dropped the knife, leaned over and pushed him under the water with her forward hooves. Holding his head down until he stopped thrashing. She reached for the knife and stabbed his floating carcass several times. She reared back, stood back up, but lost the knife in the process. It skittered off. She searched but couldn't find it. She probably wanted to carry it over to the balcony and toss it into the ocean. She shrugged drunkenly, looked around, saw no one and calmly returned to her rooms, closing the door behind her. The next images were the Twins searching for their towel animal prizes for the scavenger hunt.

Howard looked at me and the Twins who were standing goggle eyed. "Ursula, alert Octavius and the Special Agent. Gladys killed her husband. Call the Captain and security, Maury and get her in the brig."

It took a few moments to get everyone activated and it was then we discovered that Gladys, her dead mate and the lawyers were on their way to the airport and ultimately, Houston. Agent Badger called up the Grand Turk Deputy Commissioner and urgently requested him to have the pickup truck intercepted before it got to JAGS McCartney Airport. Unfortunately that was only a mile from the cruise center and the police arrived in time to see the truck on its way back and the Vaquero Oil jet lifting off from the single runway and heading out over the ocean on its way to Texas.

Rather than try to call the plane back, the FBI Agent spoke with McCartney Operations and determined that the jet had filed a flight plan for Ellington Airport, a mixed military and general aviation facility north of Houston. She contacted the FBI Field Office in Houston and had them order up a team to arrest Gladys on her arrival. They were prepared to deal with her lawyers as necessary as well as the hearse operators summoned to handle Humphrey's body.

At the Special Agent's request, the VR team forwarded a copy of the enhanced security tapes to the FBI Houston Field Office. The heifer had a lot of explaining to do.

The Purser notified the corporate management team at Solar Seas. Wally Wapiti called the Captain, the Special Agent and Octavius who filled him in on what they had discovered. Honey Badger assured him they would have Gladys in custody as soon as she arrived in Houston. Probably not without a fight.

Octavius snorted, "Let's see her *bully* her way out of this one."

The Captain laughed, "Oh, she'll try. She'll try."

Meanwhile, a tropical storm was building up off the coast of Africa and moving westward at a moderate rate. It was getting more than its fair share of attention on the *SS SOLARWIND*'s bridge.

The Captain put the command staff and crew on high alert and had security search the Cruise Center for stragglers returning from the beach, bars and shops. As soon as they were certain that all the passengers were back on board *(minus Gladys and Humphrey)* he ordered the ship to weigh anchor and head due south for the Dominican Republic and Amber Cove, 120 miles away. The dock facility there is a much safer location to ride out a storm than Grand Turk.

The Development of Civilization Volume 19 Part 4

Hurricanes, Typhoons, Tropical Cyclones, Depressions and Storms.

From "An Introduction to Faunapology"

by Octavius Bear Ph.D.

Hurricane, Typhoon, and Tropical Cyclone are different words for the same phenomena. The terms "hurricane" and "typhoon" are regionally specific names for a strong "tropical cyclone".

Want a definition? OK, hold your breath. A tropical cyclone is the generic term for a non-frontal, synoptic scale (600 to 1200 miles in length) low-pressure system over tropical or sub-tropical waters with organized convection. (i.e. thunderstorm activity) and definite cyclonic surface wind circulation (Holland 1993).

Right, Let's simplify that. Here's what NOAA (National Oceanic and Atmospheric Administration) has to say:

Tropical cyclones with maximum sustained surface winds of less than 39 mph are usually called "tropical depressions" Once the tropical cyclone reaches winds of at least 39 mph it is typically called a "tropical storm" and is assigned a name. If winds reach 74 mph, the terms differ depending on geography:

- *"hurricane" (the North Atlantic Ocean, the Northeast Pacific Ocean east of the dateline, or the South Pacific Ocean east of 160°E)*

- *"typhoon" (the Northwest Pacific Ocean west of the dateline)*

- *"severe tropical cyclone" or "Category 3 cyclone" and above (the Southwest Pacific Ocean west of 160°E or Southeast Indian Ocean east of 90°E)*

- *"very severe cyclonic storm" (the North Indian Ocean)*

- *"tropical cyclone" (the Southwest Indian Ocean)*

So. what you call it depends on where you are but the damaging effects are the same.

How Do Hurricanes Form? <small>(Courtesy of University Corporation for Atmospheric Research (UCAR) Center for Science Education and Wikipedia)</small>

Thunderstorms, warm ocean water and light winds are the conditions needed for a hurricane to form. Once formed, a hurricane consists of huge rotating rain bands with a center of clear skies called the eye which is surrounded by the fast winds of the eyewall. Here's an example:

Off the west coast of Africa, just north of the equator, a thunderstorm forms. It is just a typical towering thunderstorm cloud, but it might grow into something quite different — a hurricane.

Perhaps several other thunderstorms form in the same area. And perhaps all those dark towering thunderstorm clouds begin to rotate around an area of low atmospheric pressure called a tropical depression. Drawing enough energy from the warmth of the tropical ocean water, these circling thunderstorms might grow into a single tropical storm with winds blowing more than 39 miles per hour. If it grows even larger and winds swirl faster than 74 miles per hour, it is called a hurricane.

This happens in many other warm, tropical areas of the world too, but only under certain circumstances. For one to form, there needs to be warm ocean water and moist, humid air in the region. When humid air is flowing upward at a zone of low pressure over warm ocean water, the water is released from the air, as creating the clouds of the storm.

As it rises, the air in a hurricane rotates. Air drawn into the center of a hurricane curves to the right in the Northern Hemisphere and toward the left in the Southern Hemisphere due to the Coriolis effect — a phenomenon in which winds curve because of the Earth's rotation. At lower latitudes, where there is no Coriolis effect, hurricanes cannot form within 300 miles (500 kilometers) of the equator.

Storms grow if there is a continuous supply of energy from warm ocean water and warm, moist air. Tropical storms can grow into hurricanes, and hurricanes can grow into stronger hurricanes. However, only a small number of storms grow into tropical storms. Even fewer become hurricanes.

Storms weaken when they move over areas with cooler ocean water. There isn't nearly as much energy in the water to fuel the storm, nor is there as much humidity in the air. Hurricanes also weaken when they travel over land.

So, What Does a Storm Need to Form and Grow?

1. *Hurricanes take energy from the warm ocean water to become stronger. While a hurricane is over warm water it will continue to grow.*
2. *Because of low pressure at its center, winds flow toward the center of the storm and air is forced upward. High in the atmosphere, winds flow away from the storm, which allows more air from below to rise.*
3. *The air that rises needs to be warm and moist so that it forms the clouds of the storm. Warm, moist air is found above warm, tropical ocean waters.*
4. *A hurricane also needs the winds outside the storm to be light. These winds steer the storm but are not strong enough to disrupt it.*

As a storm grows, it goes through a series of stages. First, it starts as a tropical disturbance. Then, with cyclonic circulation and faster wind speeds, it becomes a tropical depression. If the wind keeps getting faster it becomes a tropical storm and then a hurricane if winds are more than 74 miles per hour. The classifications are based on the wind speeds in the storm, not the size of the storm. Hurricanes that look small on radar can have very high wind speeds, and large storms can have low wind speeds. Hurricanes can spawn local tornadoes.

Don't confuse these storms with tornadoes, waterspouts or monsoons. A tornado is a narrow, violently rotating column of air over land that extends from a thunderstorm to the ground, not water. Tornadoes are among the most destructive phenomena of all atmospheric storms we experience

Waterspouts are essentially tornadoes that arise over water or migrate there from land. The Florida Atlantic coast and Great Lakes are two US sites where waterspouts frequently occur.

A monsoon is a seasonal period of heavy rains especially in the South Pacific and Indian Ocean.

On board the SS SOLARWIND, we'll sit at the Amber Cove slip and hope the tropical disturbance holds at that level and resists any temptation to increase its speed and violence.

Chapter Seven

Gladys' plane descends out of the sky.
It's detained by the swift FBI.
She is under arrest
And quite sorely distressed.
Most of Texas can hear her shrill cry.

Meanwhile, at Ellington Airport outside Houston, the Vaquero Oil jet was directed off the runway to a staging area where several FBI SUVs were waiting. The pilot announced the diversion as they taxied to their destination. "Sorry folks but it seems we are going to be boarded by a contingent of FBI agents. I have no choice but to comply."

The two lawyers were shocked but Gladys went ballistic. "What is this all about, Max? You're my lawyer. Deal with it. Isn't it bad enough Humphrey is dead. Am I going to be harassed by the Feds. You, Esther. Get me off this plane! Pilot! Don't you dare open the door and let them in. I'll have you and your crew all fired."

As the jet's engines went silent, the vehicles moved in front and behind the stopped aircraft. The flight attendant lowered the airstairs to the screams of the heifer. "Let me out of here!"

Three agents *(German Shepherds)* brandishing weapons climbed up the stairs, passing the attendant. The pilot and co-pilot remained locked in the cockpit. The agents ignored the two lawyers and headed immediately to the cow who was cursing and attempting to break out of her seating arrangement. She lunged at the lead agent and he growled at her. "Gladys Vaquero, you are under arrest for the murder of your husband Humphrey Vaquero. You have the right to remain silent. Anything you say can and will be used against you in a court of law. You have the right to an attorney. If you cannot afford an attorney, one will be provided for you. Do you understand the rights I have just read to you? With these rights in mind, do you wish to speak to me?"

"Get away from me, you fathead. I have nothing to say to you and my lawyers are sitting right there. Talk to them."

Needless to say, Max and Esther were shocked. They introduced themselves while Gladys remained screaming and lowing. "What is this all about, agent? Murder? Mrs. Vaquero? Surely a mistake."

"No mistake, counsellor. We have ample evidence showing your client in the act of killing her husband in the VIP Pool on the *SS SOLARWIND* on the high seas. We'll show it to you in due course. The ship is American flagged so we have jurisdiction and we have a Special Agent on board who will be in charge of our investigation and prosecution."

Gladys screamed, "Lies. It's a frameup. They have no evidence. That lousy cruise company is behind this. I'll ruin them all."

Max turned to the cow and said, "Gladys. Hold your tongue before you say something incriminating. Go with the agents. We'll see what we can do about getting you out on bail." Esther nodded in agreement.

The agent barked. "This is a capital Federal offense, counsellor. Bail may be difficult to come by. Come along Mrs. Vaquero. Are we going to have to restrain you?"

The cow collapsed and passed out. She'd been downing alcohol all the way up on the trip and giving the flight attendant plenty of abuse in the process. The three dogs and the attendant wrestled her to her hooves and struggled to get her down the airstairs and locked into the back of an oversized van. The lawyers rode along with her on their way to the Field Office confinement facility.

Max Marshall sat thinking whether the Vaquero Oil account was worth all this hassle. Unfortunately, this would not be the right time to resign their representation. He shrugged. The Eagle fluttered her wings. In the back, Gladys Vaquero snored.

*****

Belinda took Harriet, the cruise columnist, aside and cautioned her about how she reported Humphrey's death and Gladys' apparent guilt. She could taint the trial proceedings. Harriet protested that every day broadsheets and tabloids alike reported on murders. The public needed to know. The rest of the ship's passengers needed to know. Belinda decided to leave it up to the

Chief Purser to deal with the newshound and returned to her bowl of champagne. Yet another storm at sea. Her experience with Australian monsoons were quite enough, thank you. Of course, a ship this size secured at a dock with its engines at the ready to offset the heavy winds would be another story. She hoped.

*****

The storm, a 42 mph tropical depression at the moment, was due to arrive at about 9 PM. The crew was busy emptying the pools, stowing deck furniture, covering open areas, lowering the windsails, securing antennas and other projections, sealing windows and balconies, double checking the engines and getting all hands into emergency mode. The kitchens shut down the stoves and ranges. Passengers were required to secure all loose objects in their rooms that could fall, vibrate or break as the ship began to rock in the gusting winds.

Belinda and Chita, polished off another round of champagne. The cat looked at the Bearoness and me and said, "Belinda, Maury, you know what I hate more than water? Water that's flying around at high speed. What's this Amber Cove like anyway?"

I replied, "It's supposed to be state of the art but we'll probably never find out. Oh well, any port in a storm, I suppose. I should have stayed in Cincinnati."

The restaurants and bars remained open but served their cold wares on plastic dishes and tumblers. The social directress was organizing games and diversions, especially for the youngsters. Bearnice was leading a karaoke session in one of the lounges and Madame Giselle and Otto were setting up to do one of their shows in the main theatre. Staff Captain Montmorency was going from deck to deck checking and inspecting.

The VR room was shut down and all electronic games turned off. The Twins were desolate but they soldiered on developing the plot of *Bears at Sea* on their portable laptops.

Down on decks One and Zero, Chief Engineer Pruitt Pronghorn and his staff were checking the engines, generators, batteries and the server farm. Communications were tested and retested. Internet and passenger phone use was limited. With the wind and sun sails retracted, they were going to rely on the LNG powered engines to keep a flow of electricity going through the ship. Non-essential power hogs like the laundry and freight elevators were shut down. Since they were in port, the casino was closed. The Captain decided to close down the shops much to the chagrin of the female passengers.

*****

Storm or no storm, the show must go on. Promptly at eight, the house lights in the packed Tropical Theatre dimmed and a drum roll grew in volume and speed. Otto "zapped' onstage from nowhere and executed a series of backflips ending in a kneeling bow with arms spread as the brass exploded with an exciting fanfare. Ta-Da! Wild applause. "How did he do that? Where did he come from?" The Octavians knew, The tourists didn't.

"Ladies and Gentlebeasts," he shouted, "Welcome to the *SS SOLARWIND Tropical Theatre.* I am obviously not Madame Giselle. *(Laughter)* As you've probably concluded, I am Hairy Otter, known in some circles as Sir Otto the Magnificent. We're delighted you've chosen to join us this evening where we are prepared to awe you and entertain you."

He bowed again and straightened his red satin jacket. "Now, let me introduce the mysterious mistress of cartomancy, Madame Giselle, Queen of the Tarot."

The band played an exotic oriental melody as Giselle made her entrance, bathed in a following spotlight. Clad in a sparkling gold lamé robe with a small matching turban perched between her ears, she bowed to the audience's enthusiastic applause, nodded to Otto and proceeded to the elaborately decorated table and chairs positioned in the center of the stage. Once she was seated, Otto looked at her and asked, "Madame, are the spirits active tonight?"

"Mais Oui, Monsieur Otto. In spite of the storm, they are quite eager to help our friends reach new wisdom."

"Well, let's begin!"

"Will you fetch the cards for me please?"

Suddenly a cascade of cards *(under Otto's telekinetic control)* tumbled out of the air and landed in a neat stack in front of the Bichon. (Ooohs and aaahs from the audience.)

She barked, "Very clever, Mon Ami. Shall I do a quick reading for you?"

"Of course, make a prediction."

"First you must cut and shuffle the cards."

The deck rose from the table, broke into two halves, shuffled itself and settled back on the surface, face down. *(Amazed laughter)*

He chortled, "There! So much easier to let them do it themselves. You know what a klutz I am."

"Indeed, let me take a moment to explain the Tarot deck for those in the audience who are not familiar with it." She gave a short tutorial and then waved Otto into the other chair.

"You have just returned from several journeys, am I correct?"

"Unfortunately, yes!"

"Let us see if the cards have anything to say about that. As you know, the Tarot is also known as the Fool's Journey.."

"Well, I'm certainly the Fool."

"I shall take 3 cards." She flipped the top card. "Indeed, you are. Here is the Fool. Let us take the next card. Ah. The Chariot. Your journey begins. And now The third Card The Wheel of Fortune. Are you ready to embark and bring fortune with you?"

He disappeared. *(zapped)* Murmurs throughout the audience. Suddenly a squeaky voice resonated from the back of the room. "Here I am, Madame. Journey's end. I have your first seeker ready to join you. Come with me, Miss."

He led a slender female gazelle up to the stage. "Madame *Giselle.* This is Ms. Zelda *Gazelle*. She seeks your guidance."

"Thank you, Otto. Please be seated Ms. Gazelle. Have we ever met or do we have mutual acquaintances?"

"Er, No! I just arrived today. This is my first cruise. I don't know either of you."

"D'accord!" A message flashed across her contact lenses. Ursula 17 on the job. "She's a data specialist on vacation, by herself and looking for romance."

"Am I correct that you are here alone?"

"Yes! I'm on vacation."

"Away from all those databases, computers and annoying software."

"How did you know I'm involved in databases?"

"The spirits informed me. Now let us see what is in store for you."

She handed the deck to the gazelle who rather skillfully cut and shuffled the cards and gave them back.

Giselle chuckled. "I see you are a card player." She peeled off and laid out three cards. She turned them over slowly and said, "I see an important change in your life. A pleasant change. You will find romance soon."

Zelda gasped, clasped Giselle's paw and stepped backward on the stage. Otto was on the side of the room with a large antelope male in tow. Madame Giselle, meet Mister Antwell. Ursula flashed on Giselle's contact lenses. "Single, rich, stockbroker, British aristocracy, son of an earl, socially unskilled."

"Bon Soir, Monsieur or should I call you Milord? You are the son of an earl, are you not."

He reacted in amazement. "It's true but I don't use the title. Actually I'm a second son."

"But your elder brother is no longer alive?"

"Unfortunately, no!"

"So Milord, What can the spirits help you with?"

"I don't know. I'd just like something new in my life."

"Perhaps, *someone* new?"

"Well, yes!"

"Let us see!" She handed him the deck which he also skillfully shuffled and cut.

Otto chuckled. "Had some experience with cards, eh?"

"A bit." He placed the deck face down and Giselle picked off the top three cards.

"It seems you have attracted the ladies. The Queen of Wands, the Queen of Swords and the Empress. All good signs of a blossoming relationship."

Otto leaned over and said. "May I introduce you two. Your lordship, meet Zelda. Zelda meet the Earl. You're both a pair of cardsharps." Laughter and applause as the two of them left the stage.

And so it went. Otto amazing the audience with his slapstick tricks, Giselle pretending annoyance at his antics and reading the Tarot cards for six or seven more members of the audience.

Outside the wind was picking up and rain began to spatter on the decks and bulkheads. Louella was on her way. Up on the bridge and down in the engine room, activity was at a peak. In the theatre, fun and games was still the rule.

Finally the band started to play Giselle's exit music. She rose and bowed. "Mesdames and Messieurs. Merci Beaucoup. My associate and I are so pleased that you have joined us this evening. I hope you feel the spirits made our little offering entertaining and valuable. Please join us again. We perform four nights a week here and in the show lounges. I can be reached by appointment as well. Thank you again. Au Revoir. Be careful during the storm. Say goodnight, Otto!"

"Goodnight Otto!" Hairy Otter sent the Tarot deck flying into the air, executed several back flips and caught the cards in a stack before they fell to the floor. The crowd went wild.

A standing ovation as the two of them took several bows while the band continued to play their exit music. The Twins mobbed her. "We need to get you two in our new game, *Bears at Sea*. You'll be a smash. We can start work on your avatars as soon as the Virtual Reality room comes back up."

Otto laughed. Giselle looked puzzled. "What's an avatar?"

"It originally meant the Hindu representation of a god. Now, it's an electronic image that represents a computer user that may be manipulated in a game or on the internet.

"Somebody is going to manipulate me? No thank you."

"No, no." said Arabella, "You use the avatar to represent yourself in Virtual Reality. Other people have their own avatars. Your character performs in the game according to the avatar's personality. In your case, you're a brilliant seer who gives advice and warnings. Otto is your assistant who clowns around but is super capable. The two of you are a formidable pair. In other words. You are who you really are. Madame Giselle and her wonderful sidekick."

The Bichon was still dubious. "I want to see this before I say yes. What do you think, Otto?"

"We determine what the avatar says and does. They don't control us. At least I think so. Oh, what the heck. It sounds like a great spoof and you know me for spoofing."

"That's what has me worried. You're bad enough in the real world. What will you be like in Virtuous Reality."

"Virtual Reality!"

"That's what I said."

The Twins broke up. "Oh, you two are great! This will be our best game yet. We have to work in this storm and the dead bull that we discovered. The gamester geeks at the Hex are going to go crazy over this one. *Blockbuster Bears at Sea*! Yes!

They ran off to start work on their laptops.

Chapter Eight

Louella, the storm's on her way.
SOLARWIND battens down for the fray.
Though they're tied to a slip
There's concern on the ship.
Will the tempest result in dismay?

A series of musical notes sounded throughout the ship. An official announcement. "Attention, please. All passengers and crew! This is the Captain speaking. As we have told you earlier , Tropical Storm Louella is making its way toward the Dominican Republic. It is packing winds of up to 70 miles an hour. Just short of a hurricane. We are safely moored at a slip here in Amber Cove. But we will be riding out some heavy downpours and blows. I hope you have all followed our instructions about securing all loose items that could cause damage or injury. We are running checks of the cabins right now. We have curtailed a number of services either to reduce threats or conserve power. We have also secured as many articles of furniture and machinery on the decks as is possible. Sorry for the inconveniences but your safety is our number one concern."

"Since we have had to retract our wind and sun sails, we have been using the engines to generate electric power to the ship. However, we now need them to maintain stability and keep station here at the Amber Cove slip. Our batteries are now fully charged and we will be cutting over to them in a few minutes. When that happens, the entire ship will go dark momentarily except for our exit and safety lights. Power will return in short order as we complete the transition. Before that period of darkness, you are requested to find a safe location, stay calm and avoid movement. Parents, please ensure all children are relaxed and secure. Under no circumstances, go out on any of the decks. We expect the storm to last several hours and we will continue to brief you on its progress and our status. Thank you all for your cooperation and continued loyalty to Solar Seas Company."

"We will make the transition in ten minutes. We will count down at that time. Please settle yourselves and stand by for further instructions."

Needless to say, a number of enterprising passengers flocked to the bars to replenish their drinks. Sofas, banquettes and other public seating was at a premium. The elevators and stairwells were filled with individuals trying to return to their cabins. The crew had their paws full maintaining order but fortunately there was no real panic.

The Octavians came together as a group. They had been in the Tropical Theatre to watch and applaud Madame Giselle and Sir Otto the Magnificent. Octavius and Bel's Imperial Suite was just one deck above the theatre and the group tried to reach the suite but found the stairs and elevators clogged. They sat back down in the theatre and waited for the lights to go out. The twins were busy with their laptops and the self-powered Ursulas were keeping track of the storm's intensity and progress. Meanwhile the wind started to howl in earnest, rain spattered torrentially against the windows, portholes, doors and balconies. Some swinging projections banged against the walls and bulkheads. The storm had arrived.

The Captain came back on the speakers. *"Thank you once again for your attention and cooperation. You can no doubt, hear, feel and perhaps see the effects of the storm. We will safely ride it out here in port. The ship will be in darkness for only a few brief moments while we switch to battery power. We are counting down. Ten-nine-eight-seven-six-five-four-three-two-one."*

Darkness descended throughout the ship. broken only by the emergency lights. Nervous laughter in the theatre. A few idiots in the bars screamed, shouted or uttered ghostly moans and groans. The outage lasted less than a minute.

The lights and air conditioning stuttered back on. One scream was not phony. A well dressed female goat lay prone and unconscious in a passageway outside the theatre. Belinda spotted her and rushed to her side, calling for security and a doctor. A nurse arrived first and worked to revive the nanny. She slowly came around, looked at Belinda and promptly fainted again at the sight of the large polar sow.

The nurse asked the Bearoness to step away. "She's out of it, my lady. Something really scared her." Belinda backed up a few steps.

Octavius took his cue from his mate and stood to the side as the nurse worked to once again resuscitate the goat. She awoke, shook her head and bleated. "Oh, I'm so sorry. I was struck and knocked down. I guess I fainted. She looked over at Belinda, smiled weakly and said, "Goodness, Bearoness, you scared me. Waking up and finding a polar bear holding my hoof. Sorry, this nanny is a ninny. I'm Cassandra Caprine. Everybody calls me Cassy."

Belinda laughed, "Don't concern yourself. We polars can be scary. Are you all right?"

"I think so, my head and neck hurts. Wait! Where is my diamond necklace?"

Two young goats, a doe and a billy, rushed up. "Mom. Mom. What happened? "

"I was attacked. Someone took my pendant."

Dudley Diomede, the Albatross Chief Security Officer, arrived with Doctor Goro. He checked the goat over and treated her bruised neck. "Just a couple of minor bruises, Mrs. Caprine, but what's this about being attacked and having your necklace stolen?"

"I was and it is. It's a 5 carat, emerald cut diamond solitaire on a white gold chain.. It was a first anniversary present from my mate, the billionaire Casper Caprine. He died last year in a climbing accident. It's very valuable and heavily insured but more important, it has great sentimental value. I knew I shouldn't have worn it but I do so love it."

Her two children helped her to her feet. "Thank you, Carson. Don't start sniveling, Cassidy. I'm quite all right. The doctor said so but"- she turned to the security officer- "what about my necklace? Can you get it back and arrest the thief?"

"We'll do our best, madam." He looked at Octavius who nodded his head. "We have a group of top notch detectives on board. I'll ask them to take up the case."

Belinda rolled her eyes and murmured. "Here we go again. He just can't resist."

*****

Tropical Storm Louella shook, rattled and rolled her rain-filled way across the island of Hispaniola leaving Haiti and the Dominican Republic worse for wear and tear. Downed trees, torn roofs, debris, floating furniture, broken windows, fallen wire, intermittent floods, swamped cars, communications and power outages in many areas. Thank goodness, no fatalities or serious injuries. Had it reached hurricane status, the results would have been far more devastating. As it was, there was a lot of expensive, time consuming and frustrating repair and recovery work that needed to be done.

The **SS Solarwind** 'weathered' the storm in stalwart fashion, losing several antennas, flooded decks and balconies, and a few broken windows and doors but nothing that could not be rapidly repaired. One exception: two solar/wind sails were damaged even though they had been retracted. That would require special repairs back at Fort Lauderdale. After the brunt of the tempest passed and the winds subsided to a more rational speed, the Chief Engineer raised the remaining eight functioning sails and switched back from battery to wind/sun power. They would also recharge the batteries. The engines reverted to Liquid Natural Gas and were readied for propulsion.

The Captain decided the damage at Amber Cove was too severe to allow shore parties. The Cruise Center facilities were all closed and repair and recovery work was in process. The ship had lost a day already and having to move more slowly, would be falling further behind in the 14 day itinerary. He decided to lift anchor, bypass Grand Cayman which had sustained even greater damage from the storm and move on to Cozumel circumventing Belize. He planned an extra day in Cozumel to compensate. Louella had turned north-eastward back to sea and Mexico had escaped the blow. Needless to say, there were murmurings, complaints and groans from the passengers but an act of nature needed to be accommodated.

(Thank goodness the Vaqueros were no longer aboard. Gladys was far too busy at the moment in Houston trying to stay out of jail. Because of the storm, she probably would have attempted to sue the ship, staff and crew, the cruise line, and the weather services. If not God.)

The Purser and Social Directress were operating at "full speed plus" and the crew was working around the clock to restore all of the ships' facilities and amenities. Giselle, Otto, Belinda, Bearyl and Bearnice were among the guests who volunteered to provide additional entertainment. Chita and Lepi had the younger show lounge set eating out of their paws with their rocking sets and wild driving solos. The rest of us, Maury *(me)*, Howard, Frau Ilse, the Colonel, Ben and Gal (the Flying Tigers), Lord David, Dancing Dan and Jaguar Jack, offered our services to the Bridge.

The casino was reopened, the swim pools refilled and the bars and restaurants fully operational. Fortunately the kitchen supplies and liquid reserves had been topped up at Grand Turk. The shops were doing land office business. Karaoke and all sorts of participatory games were in full swing. The VR room was open and the Twins had converted two of their games to Virtual Reality along with several others. Books from the ship's library disappeared. Every effort was being made to keep the tourists occupied, satisfied and distracted. Except for a certain female goat who was sore distressed on the loss of her high value bauble.

Security Chief Diomede had his staff interviewing those passengers who had been in or near the theatre when the lights went out. Thus far, no joy. A few remembered the fainting goat but no one could shed any light *(pun intended)* on what happened when the ship had gone dark.

*****

Frau Ilse came up to Octavius and said, "We have a surprise. Guess who's been on board and managing the exclusive high end jewelry shop."

The Great Bear, who was not fond of guessing games, growled "Who?"

"Mister Alex of Alexandria. You remember our civet friend from Washington who helped us with the Attaché Case. *(See Book 6)* It seems in addition to his international boutiques, he has shops on several cruise

77

ships. **SS Solarwind** is his latest venue. He's here to kick the relationship off. Chita will be delighted. She's an old customer of his. I invited him to join us in your suite."

Mister Alex had analyzed a collection of smuggled uncut diamonds for us and confirmed that they were 'blood diamonds' intended to support an African revolution. Octavius, the Frau, the Colonel and I had used his input to solve a killing of an attaché impala at an embassy and ultimately put paid to an international scandal.

Octavius turned to me and said, "Maury, by all means, let's gather the clan and greet our comrade. Tell Carlos to put together snacks and drinks."

The civet, dressed in his tail coat arrived and was effusive in his greetings which the Frau and Chita reciprocated. Belinda, resplendent in her bejeweled finery, was introduced along with the rest of the Octavians. The Great Bear, the Colonel and I recalled the final solution to the Attaché incident, which Mr. Alex had never heard. "I'm delighted I could be of service. Perhaps I can be again."

Octavius looked at him quizzically. "How so?"

"This goat who was struck down and had her 5 carat, emerald cut diamond solitaire lifted during the brief blackout. Are you working on that case?

"Yes, we are."

"Well, you should know that bauble of hers is synthetic. Still a true diamond but far less valuable than she has made it out to be."

"How do you know that?"

"I sold it to Casper Caprine for their first anniversary. He managed to insure it as if it were a natural diamond. Way overvalued! Insurance companies weren't as aware of the distinction in those days. and the diamond had all the top ratings for color, clarity, cut and carat. But, if they pay up, Mrs. Caprine will get a significant windfall. She can't resell it for anywhere near its insured value."

"She says the loss is primarily sentimental."

"Maybe! Maybe not! Anyway, a little advertising. Ladies, please come to the Alex Sea Boutique. You'll be delighted."

The Development of Civilization Volume 19 Part 5
Lab Grown Diamonds and Gemstones.

From "An Introduction to Faunapology"

by Octavius Bear Ph.D.

My wife and companion of many years is, among her many talents, a glamorous showbear aqueuse as well as a very rich member of Scottish nobility. Both of these characteristics have allowed her to develop a strong and affectionate relationship with expensive jewelry – most often diamonds and gold. Our colleague, Chita, Madame Catt, is also a lapidary enthusiast and perpetually sports a diamond collar of great beauty and worth.

They have both been heard on occasion singing, "Diamonds are a girl's best friend." I take exception to that thought but my protests have been summarily ignored. I am very much in a male minority, eschewing jewelry, although I must admit that much of Bearoness Belinda's hoard has come from me in my weaker moments. The sources of Chita's adornments are known only to the Cat herself.

For millions of years, diamonds have taken form in underground depths under immense pressure and then waited for enterprising (and often ruthless) animals to dig them up, shape and polish them and foist their sparkling and dazzling forms on a public willing to pay outlandish prices to possess them. Rarity and cost have created a mystique around diamonds and other uncommon gemstones and launched and grown highly lucrative industries in mining, cutting, polishing, wholesale and retail. Recently the characteristics of those industries have changed.

Enter synthetic and simulated diamonds and gemstones! A lab grown diamond is one that has been manufactured in a controlled environment. Lab-Grown Diamonds (also known as lab created diamonds, manufactured diamonds, man-made diamonds, engineered diamonds, and cultured diamonds) still only occupy a very small segment of the market. But that segment is growing for several reasons.

First: Lab-grown diamonds are true diamonds in physical, chemical, optical and atomic structure. They have shape, size, color and clarity grades, just like Natural Diamonds. They have exactly the same hardness level and durability.

Second: Using Chemical Vapor Deposition (CVD) or High Pressure High Temperature (HPHT), scientists can now create diamonds that optically look like earth-mined diamonds, contain the same chemical and physical attributes and even receive certification through the Gemological Institute of America (GIA) and International Gemological Institute (IGI). They are just as real as diamonds that are mined from the earth.

The differences between Natural Diamonds and Lab Grown Diamonds cannot be seen with the naked eye. Natural Diamonds contain tiny amounts of nitrogen, while Lab Grown Diamonds do not. This is actually one of the signifiers gemologists use to identify if a diamond is lab grown or natural. When it comes to grading Lab Grown Diamonds, the same 4 Cs: Color, Cut, Clarity and Carat are applied. Time is of the essence. In fact, the process used to create a Lab Grown Diamond cuts down the grow time significantly, from millions of years to a couple of months. Then, the Lab Diamond is also cut and polished.

The third difference is becoming the most powerful. Lab diamonds are significantly less expensive than natural diamonds and showing even more attractive pricing. However, resale values may be correspondingly very low.

Finally, not all synthetic diamonds are gems. Much of the synthetic output ends up in industrial applications especially abrasives and electronics.

There is some argument as to whether lab diamonds are more ecologically beneficial. While they make the mining process unnecessary, they require major supplies of electricity to create the jewels, much more than is used in processing natural diamonds. And of course, mining companies and their economic contributions will be affected over time.

<u>Synthetic vs. Simulated:</u> We have thus far described synthetic diamonds. Simulated diamonds are different. The most familiar names for the simulated gems are cubic zirconia, synthetic moissanite and synthetic rutile. Some simulants have more fire than diamonds. While cubic zirconia has a wonderful shine, it does not always maintain its color and clarity over time. The chemical composition is porous, so the stone is vulnerable to pollution or contaminants in the environment. This will cause the stone to cloud and discolor, gradually fading from brilliant whiteness to a muddy yellow or brown. Although cubic zirconia may start as hard and bright, it doesn't always stay that way. Cubic zirconia stones are prone to chipping.

<u>Other synthetic gemstones:</u> A synthetic gem is one that is made in a laboratory, but which shares virtually all chemical, optical, and physical characteristics of its natural mineral counterpart. The most common are rubies, sapphires, emeralds and opals. The production processes are different but all involve a laboratory environment. Many synthetic gems finish up in class rings or costumes.

It is important to be able to distinguish the natural from synthetic products not only for economic and ethical reasons but to maintain stability and fair competition in the industries. It will take time for synthetics and simulants to capture a substantial portion of the market but trends are moving in that direction. Price differentials will become more powerful in times of inflation. World situations and such issues as 'blood diamonds' are making natural gems less desirable. Diamonds may be a girl's best friend but which ones?

Chapter Nine

The problem is just as we feared.
The large diamond has just disappeared.
When the lights all went out
It was gone. Not a doubt!
It's a theft that is certainly weird.

Trying to get a lead on the missing diamond, Frau Ilse, Lord David and I set about interviewing the three goats. We had an Ursula with us. We decided to do it individually starting with Carson, the young billy. We took up the same office that Special Agent Badger had been using while she managed the inquiry into Humphrey Vaquero's death. Carson was a full size black and tan but still developing. I suspect he would be very attractive to many a doe. I led off. Two foot tall, unimposing me.

"Carson, do you mind if I call you Carson?"

"That's my name. Be my guest."

I smiled "We've been asked by the Captain to help track down your mother's diamond necklace and find the thief who attacked her. What can you tell us that will move our search along."

"Nothing really. Cassidy and I were in the nearby show lounge listening to your buddies, Chita and Lepi, when the lights went out. Those two are rad."

'I know. I'm their agent."

"Cool! Can you get us autographs?"

"Sure, but let's get back to the attack."

"Mom was in the theatre watching those mystics. Not Cassidy's or my thing. We only found out about what happened to her when the power came back on. She was flat out on the floor with a polar bear and a nurse working on her. She was bleating about her stolen necklace."

"What about the necklace."

"It's a bigass diamond she got from my father. She wears it all the time. Says it reminds her of him. Frankly, I think it's gross. I suppose it's worth a lot. I never asked. It was only a matter of time before it got stolen but I never expected someone to slug her and rob her in the dark."

"Has the diamond ever been stolen before?"

"It went missing once for a couple of days. She forgot to put it in the safe and a maid picked it up and shoved it in a drawer and went off for the weekend. All sorts of upset until the maid returned and brought it out. But no, there were never any break-ins or thefts."

The Frau asked. "Why are you three on this cruise."

"Cassidy's birthday present. She leaves for college when we return. I just graduated. I'll be joining my dead father's business when we get back. Mom is on the board."

Lord David asked, "What business is that?"

"Caprine Associates. Venture capital. Investments. We have a piece of some unicorns."

The Frau raised her wolfish eyebrows. "Unicorns? The horses with the spiral horns?"

He bleated and rolled his eyes. "Naah! In business, a unicorn is a privately held startup company worth over a billion dollars. Like the horse, they're pretty rare. We manage a few of them and own one or two. I'll be running a couple."

She smiled. "I learn something new every day. Is there anything else you can tell us?

He bleated again. "Nope. Hope you find the robber and that damned diamond. Actually, I wish she'd get rid of it. Stupid thing. Maybe you won't find it and she can get the insurance."

I said, "Well we're trying. Thanks Carson. Can you send in your sister?"

"If I can find the lazy thing."

He left and the three of us stared at each other. Lord David spoke. "I think he knows more than he's saying but I have a suspicious mind.

The Frau agreed and I made it unanimous. "Ursula. How about looking up Caprine Associates. Let's see what we can learn about those unicorn herders."

"I'm on it, Maury."

We waited for Cassidy to make her appearance and mused about the three goats. Something seemed off but we didn't have enough evidence to go on. Meanwhile, ship security and the rest of the Octavians were seeking out any and all of the folks who were in the vicinity when the assault and robbery took place. Still nothing. Mr. Alex's revelation had Octavius doing research on lab grown diamonds. Belinda, Chita, Giselle and Gal were doing research on Mr. Alex's shop. The Blanc sisters, Bearyl and Bearnice, oddly enough, were not jewelry enthusiasts. Neither is the Frau.

A knock on the door and a pure white doe poked her head into the room. "Hi, I'm Cassidy Caprine. My brother says you want to talk to me."

I did the introductions and asked the same questions about the event. Same result. Cassidy was a bit of an airhead and spent much of the time talking about her birthday and college plans. She didn't seem overly concerned about what had happened to her mother. She hadn't been there. As we expected, she liked the diamond and hoped to inherit it but didn't seem overly anxious about its return. She had no idea what it was worth. As far as the business went, her only concern was whether her tuition and expenses would be taken care of. In short, a spoiled kid *(no pun)* up to her chinny chin-chin in entitlement.

We thanked her and asked her to find her mother. She seemed somewhat put out by the request but shrugged and said she'd find out if she had recovered and was up to being interviewed. Back later!

*****

We decided to go to lunch. Howard, Otto, Giselle, the Colonel, Ben and Gal, Dancing Dan, Jaguar Jack, Chita and Lepi all joined us. Before we could get our orders off, Octavius, Belinda and the Twins arrived. Several Ursulas were in the party. Hail, hail, the gangs etc. etc.!

While we were choosing from the extensive menu, Jaguar Jack spoke up. "Amigos! I have news. As I was working with the security team this morning I spotted an old acquaintance of mine. Octavius knows that in an earlier life, I was known to engage in a little larceny and naughtiness. Not unlike you, my little meerkat chum." *(See Book One)*

(I waved. As a very young pup, I belonged to a jewel thieving meerkat gang on the island of Mauritius. I was the lookout for the group and was caught by Octavius plying my criminal trade. He gave me a choice. Go to a miserable jail or sign on with him and go straight. Guess what I did. Anyway, I'm interrupting Jack.)

He continued, "This guy, a coyote named Ivor, pretended he didn't know me but he is one of the most notorious pickpockets and purse snatchers anywhere in the States and South America. I passed him off to the security team and they are doing a number on him. He's using a phony name and ID. Charlie Coyote! Ha! He swears he knows nothing about the missing diamond but right now, he's being carefully scrutinized and may be on his way to the brig. I'm surprised he's out of jail and on the loose. You may want to have a chat, Octavius."

This caused a stir among the Octavians. The Twins were already trying to figure out how to include Ivor in their game. The Ursulas were doing a search on him and the Colonel was up for using his persuasive techniques. I actually pitied the guy. Octavius suggested we go and visit Mr. Coyote but only after lunch. We also needed to interview the stricken widow.

*****

Back in the conference room after an overly elaborate meal, Octavius, Frau Ilse, Lord David and I were getting reorganized when an Ursula 17 rang her chime. "I have the report on Caprine Associates, the Unicorn Ranchers. It's not pretty."

The Great Bear was at full attention as were we all.

"Several of their 'can't miss' start-ups have missed badly in the last six months taking their investments and net worth with them. Caprine is struggling to keep the boat afloat. (*Sorry about that!*) Our young friend Carson is going to be stuck with a couple of very sick unicorns. Cassandra (Cassy) is on the board and a major stockholder. All of the board members are being called for additional capital. The family's posh lifestyle is probably going to take a serious hit. Miss Cassidy's enrollment in the prestigious university may be in jeopardy. Not sure they'll be able to pay their bill when they exit this ship."

The Frau got the message. "So, is it just possible that faced with financial stress, the Caprines have elected to scare up some insurance money on a jewel that has little or no resale value?"

Lord David nodded his spotted head. " I'll put some money on it. It's neater than burning down a building or wrecking a Rolls-Royce but the results are the same. Insurance fraud is insurance fraud."

Octavius held up his paws. "Let's not jump to conclusions here. I admit it's a likely scenario but she seemed genuinely shook and wounded.

The Frau snorted. "Or she's a good actress."

Before the discussion could move on there was a knock on the door. "This may be her."

It wasn't. Security Chief Diomede pushed open the entrance and flapped his wings. "Sorry to interrupt but we're not getting anywhere with this coyote pickpocket. I wonder if you could be available to use your 'interview techniques' to shake him loose."

Octavius nodded and said, "Come on, Ilse. Let's go be persuasive. Maury, you and Lord David wait here and see if Mrs. Caprine makes an appearance. Buzz me if she shows. We'll come back up. Lead on, Commander! Let's meet this Charlie Coyote or is it Ivor?"

They followed the Albatross out to the freight elevator and swooped down to the brig. Diomede returned to his seat at the table as the Frau and Octavius entered. Jaguar Jack was staring at an indignant Coyote. He yipped and growled. "How many times do I have to tell you idiots I don't know anything about a missing diamond. Who are these guys? Calling in the heavyweights, are you?"

"I'm Octavius Bear and this lovely She-wolf is Frau Ilse Schuylkill-Where. We are detectives. We have it on strong authority that in spite of your current alias, you are Ivor Coyote, a well known pickpocket and purse snatcher."

"That's a lie!

Jaguar Jack laughed. "Oh come on, amigo. You and I used to work the streets and crowds of Rio and São Paulo in Brazil and Buenos Aires in Argentina. You were the light fingered scourge of BA. After a little insistent urging by my compadre, Octavius, I went straight but you seem to be still working the trade."

Diomede squawked. "Ivor, maybe you'd like to explain the wallets, watches and handbags we found in your cabin. How come your didn't ditch them."

"You searched my cabin? I want a lawyer."

Frau Ilse laughed, "You're going to need one. Where's the diamond? You're up for assaulting a female goat, too."

"OK, I swiped some pickings from a bunch of drunk dummies when the lights went out. But I don't have any damned diamond and I've never assaulted anyone. You know that, Jack."

"The Jaguar turned to the detectives and security officer. "He's right. Violence wasn't part of our MO."

Octavius looked at the ceiling. "You're going to stick to that story, are you? We already have you for petty theft. We'll be returning your spoils to the victims. You'll be stuck here in the brig until we reach Fort Lauderdale and turn you over to the local police. Any comments."

"You're a traitorous bastard, Jack"

The Jaguar shrugged. The Great Bear looked at Diomede. You searched his cabin?"

"With the proverbial fine tooth comb. If he hid it, it's not in his cabin."

"Where is it, Ivor?"

"One more time. I don't have it. I never had it."

"OK! He's useless. Lock him up! We'll continue our inquiries but if we track that jewel back to you, Ivor, you'll wish you jumped overboard."

"Get lost, Bear! Take your wolf girlfriend and squealer cat with you."

Outside, Octavius sighed, "Well, back to the drawing boards."

The Frau asked, "You believe him?"

"Not completely but our principal job is to get that necklace back. Let's return to the conference room. Perhaps the ninny-nanny will condescend to grant us an interview."

"And tell us where the necklace went to."

"You're very suspicious of the lady, Frau Ilse."

"With good reason, Herr Bear."

Chapter Ten

Back in Houston, Ms. Gladys is stuck.
All her lawyers have run out of luck.
They were destined to fail
Getting her out on bail
And the heifer is running amok.

At the FBI Houston Field Office: Gladys Vaquero had been taken into custody after her dramatic exit from the company jet at Ellington Field. Several hours later, Special Agent Honey Badger had arrived after catching the last flight out of Grand Turk before Tropical Storm Louella hit. The lawyers from Marshall and Lore were exercising their considerable skills in trying to get their client released on bail but were unsuccessful thus far.

Gladys, suffering from a severe case of alcoholic withdrawal, was at her anti-social worst. She would sue for false arrest. The FBI collectively were Nazis. Specifically, the Houston Special Agent in Charge and Special Agent Badger were Gestapo thugs. Her lawyers were a bunch of utter incompetents. The Solar Seas Company and its ridiculous ship would both sink in a sea of litigation and personal compensation. She would take it to the Supreme Court, if necessary. Needless to say, she was getting on the nerves of law enforcement.

The Agent in Charge looked at the Badger and said, "She's all yours. She hasn't shut her mooing trap since we brought her in. Why didn't you just shove her overboard while you had the chance."

She laughed and said, "Just keep her in a cell and let her rant. I need to talk with her lawyers. I assume they're still here."

"Oh, yeah but I'll bet they want to be anywhere else but with her."

"Don't we all. Lead me to them."

The lawyers were seated in a 'Plain Jane Federal' conference room surrounded by papers, cell phones and laptop computers. Max Marshall had left the team in the capable claws of Esther Eagle. She in turn was handing out assignments to a pair of junior attorneys when Special Agent Badger knocked on the door with an agent from the Field Office in tow.

"Ah, the sea-going member of the FBI and her assistant. We're awaiting someone from the prosecutor's office but I need to talk with you."

"At your service, Counsellor. How is your client?"

"Upset!"

The Badger laughed, "Situation normal!"

"Well, yes but we're working on getting her released on bail."

"Don't hold your breath. Vicious mariticides aren't looked on too favorably by the federal courts."

"Are you kidding? Wives and husbands kill each other every day."

"By drowning and then stabbing them? Give me a break!"

"You have no admissible proof of that. That Virtual Reality show was very clever but you can't take it into court. It's highly edited fiction. That Kodiak Bear and his minions are quite skilled in creating frame-ups."

The Special Agent laughed again. "You don't have to quote us the rules of evidence, Counsellor. We have the original tapes from the ship's surveillance cameras. Unedited, timed and clearly showing your drunken, enraged client in the act of murdering her mate. We also have the knife she used with his blood and her DNA on it. Don't know why she didn't dump it over the side when she had the chance."

"Because she's not a clever murderess. She's a battered wife who defended herself against a drunken oversized bully. He struck her repeatedly. We're going to plead self-defense."

"Sure. Give it a try. But don't count on it. She's got such a big, offensive mouth, she'll talk herself into a death sentence."

One of the juniors blurted. "We don't plan to let her testify."

"Lots of luck with that, sonny. The lawyer doesn't exist who can get Gladys Vaquero to shut her trap. She'll convict herself. Can we go see her? Obviously, you'll want to be there."

The Eagle shrugged. "That's your privilege. Let's go. I'm advising her not to speak to you."

"Oh, good. That'll guarantee she'll spill her guts."

The Houston Field Office has holding cells for temporary custody of prisoners. There were still some jurisdictional questions to be ironed out before Gladys was transferred to more permanent federal facilities. International shipboard or airborne crimes presented venue and legal responsibility issues. The nationality of the victim(s) and perpetrator(s); the location of the crime (open or national waters); the registration of the ship; the ports of call.

Fortunately, this one is an all-American affair. The Vaqueros are American citizens; the ship was in open water outside any national boundary; *SS SOLARWIND*, unlike most cruise vessels, is registered in the US and the police at Grand Turk Caicos, the next port of call passed on taking on the case. Unfortunately, as far as Special Agent Badger and the Houston Agent in Charge were concerned, they were stuck with it. A Federal judge had to accept the case but probably will.

As usual, the lockups were located in a carefully secured basement of the Field Office. In spite of her lawyers' efforts, Gladys was being treated as a dangerous suspect, charged with *aggravated* murder because of the violence and so was closely confined. That didn't keep her from making maximum noise.

As the party approached her cell, the sounds of her bellowing and mooing echoed down the hallway. A female jailer stood by, clearly annoyed.

Agent Badger identified herself and her associate as well as the law team who were already known to the guard. She unlocked the door, shouting, "Gladys, you have company."

The heifer *(cow)* took up most of the cell, She looked worse for wear and suffering from nervous tremors. *(Alcohol withdrawal?)* She took one look at Honey Badger and shouted, "Get that Federal thug away from me. Just you wait, Special Agent. When I get through with you, there won't be a law office or police force that'll give you the time of day. You won't even be able to walk a beat. You're toast. Badger toast." She laughed hysterically. "Well, what are you lawyers staring at? What am I paying you for? Get me out of here. This is a frameup. I'm glad that no-good is dead but I didn't do it."

The Special Agent took all of this in and coolly replied. "We have plenty of evidence that says you did. Why don't you save yourself and the government a lot of time, energy, pain and money and confess."

The junior attorney protested. "Don't listen, Gladys!"

The cow bellowed, "Go to Hell, Badger. I'll get you like I finally got him."

Esther Eagle screeched. "Quiet, Gladys. We're pleading self-defense. Keep that in mind."

Honey Badger said, "She had motive, means and opportunity. A classic example."

"The motive was self-defense."

"No, it wasn't. Humphrey bragged to his poker mates that he was finally going to get rid of her. He was filing for a divorce that would leave her with nothing. She stupidly had signed a pre-nup agreement. He finally got his nerve up and went back to the room to deliver the bad news. Isn't that the way it was, Gladys? You were enraged and chased him with a large knife you had from room service. He ran out and drunkenly fell into the pool. You held him under till he drowned and then stabbed him multiple times for good measure."

The cow collapsed and fainted. Her lawyers looked distraught. The Special Agent turned and left with her FBI associate. "See you all in court."

Chapter Eleven

At Grand Cayman as well as Belize
The big storm brought the towns to their knees.
They were hit with great force.
So the ship changed its course
And went northward on much calmer seas.

Because of the impact of Tropical Storm Louella on the ports of call and the ship itself, Captain Lion elected to bypass heavily damaged Grand Cayman and Belize and sail for the untouched Cozumel Cruise Port. Louella had spared Mexico and steered eastward back out to sea. The Captain negotiated an early arrival and extended stay. To compensate the passengers and do some more repairs, he had decided to spend an extra day docked at the Punta Langosta Terminal adjacent to San Miguel, the island's largest city. It was no hardship for the visitors.

Cozumel lives on its tourist trade and is extremely popular with the cruise lines and their customers. Bars and restaurants abound although the ship's kitchens were laying out Mexican specialties by the ton. Tequila, margaritas and cervezas flowed lavishly.

San Miguel is a shopping paradise. Every single duty-free shop you will find in the Caribbean has at least one store in San Miguel.

Cozumel's coral reefs are some of the largest in the world. Paradise Reef and Palancar Gardens are ideal spots for novice divers and snorkelers due to their shallow depth, and offer a chance to glimpse sea turtles, colorful fish, towering coral spires, and gently waving sea fans.

The Palancar Caves are probably the most famous dive site, with huge brain corals and swim-through tunnels. Palancar Horseshoe, a natural underwater amphitheater made entirely of coral, is another must-see. Freddi Fox the Social Directress was arranging shore tours and diving expeditions. Needless to say, the Twins were signed up for snorkeling. They had become underwater addicts after their adventures at Australia's

Great Barrier Reef. Belinda decided to forgo the opportunity to swim but would not deny herself a little shopping.

Attempts to activate the two damaged wind sails went for naught due to lack of parts and repair equipment. Engineer Pruitt had been tearing up the internet getting the company's resources and maintenance crews available and prepped at Fort Lauderdale when the ship arrived. He was able to replace the lost and damaged antennas and full communications, navigation and weather systems were all restored. The Purser's staff were supervising the repairs to the deck furniture and equipment. The swimming pools were cleaned, refilled and put back in service. To the kid's delight, the zip line and carousel were active. Unfortunately or maybe not, the casino was closed. All told, it could have been a lot worse. The Staff Captain, Chief Purser and First officer were busy recording all the activities that had taken place during the storm including the arrest of the pickpocket and the mysterious disappearance of Cassandra Caprine's diamond pendant.

On that subject, Octavius, the Frau, Colonel, Lord David, Jaguar Jack and I had returned to the conference room where we were reviewing the day's interviews. A knock on the door and Cassidy Caprine poked her nose in. "My mother has agreed to see you but she's reluctant to leave her cabin. Can you come to her? My goodness, you have quite a mob here. Do you all have to question her? She's extremely uneasy."

Octavius rose to his full nine feet, head touching the ceiling in the process and startled the doe. He was not going to assuage the widow Caprine's nerves. He looked at me, the Frau and Lord David and said, "Come with me. I don't think the four of us will disturb her unduly. *(To the contrary, both he and the she wolf would intimidate anyone. However, Lord David with his spotted pelt, dignified demeanor, well-shaped ears, black nose and handsome face provided a calming effect. I was just included for comic relief.)* All right, Ms. Caprine. Lead on!"

Somewhat reluctantly, Cassidy turned and slipped out into the passageway toward the passenger elevator. Octavius reached out and said, "I'm afraid I can't join you. I can't fit in the standard elevators. I'll have to use the freight lift. What deck and cabin number is she in? I'll join you all there shortly."

This didn't raise the doe's comfort level one iota. "Luxury Deck Four, Suite Three A."

"Good. There should be plenty of room for all of us. I'll meet you there. By the way. We'd like to interview her without you or your brother being present."

She started to protest but thought better of it. She signaled for the elevator, looking suspiciously at the Frau.

The she wolf silently pondered. "Why is the doe so nervous? Wolves stopped eating goats centuries ago. Of course, Herr Bear can be scary. Guilty conscience? Well, let's see what Mama Nanny has to say for herself."

They entered the suite with an Ursula laptop in paw and found Cassandra *(call me Cassie)* lying on a chaise longue. Carson was perched on a chair opposite. Cassidy said, "Mama, these gentlebeasts want to interview you about your stolen diamond. I told them you were feeling quite upset and they said they'd be as expeditious as possible. Come, Carson. They want to be alone with Mama."

The young billy looked like he was about to object but his mother shook her head and tossed her head in the direction of the door. Her two offspring left with looks of concern on their faces. "We'll be in the deck lounge. Call us when you're through."

Frau Ilse laid the laptop with Ursula active but unnoticed on a side table. She would be recording and analyzing the event. She was still researching Caprine Associates and the dissolving unicorns. The outlook was getting worse by the minute.

I looked at the Frau and Lord David and shrugged. They shrugged back. Octavius arrived and apologized for being late. "The freight elevators are being taken up by the repair crews. The storm did some damage ship wide. Nothing serious except for two damaged wind sails and some broken antennas. The sails will have to wait till we return to Fort Lauderdale but everything else seems to be in hand."

The goat sighed, "That's a relief. I was so afraid we'd be blown over and capsized in the storm. I'm glad the Captain got us safely into port at Amber Cove. I think we've been sailing again but I've stayed in my cabin here. I'm really not an ocean person. We're on this trip for Cassidy's birthday. It's her present before she goes off to college. Have we reached Cozumel yet? Has the storm blown itself out?"

"Yes, we're at Cozumel. We're docked at San Miguel. Tropical Storm Louella has turned back out into the open sea, It missed Mexico altogether. You may wish to go ashore. Cozumel is quite an attractive island."

"I'll think abut it. Now, what did you want to ask me. I gave a complete statement to the ship's security officer, the albatross."

"Yes, we have a copy of his notes and formal report. First, how are you medically?"

"A few bruises. Nothing serious but my nerves are a mess. I've never been assaulted before. It's quite upsetting and of course, my diamond pendant is gone. Have you had any luck tracking it down?

"Not yet but we have a few leads."

"Oh yes? Well, that's encouraging! I'm so concerned."

Lord David intervened, smiling in his best doggy style. "I can imagine. Tell me, Mrs. Caprine, how much is the necklace worth?"

"Well, it's quite large. Over five carats and most highly rated by the Gemological Institute for color, cut, clarity and brilliance. I was dazzled when Casper gave it to me. Dear Casper!"

The Dalmatian did not get an answer to his question but was not going to be put off. "What's its resale value? What could the thief get for it?"

"I really don't know."

"It is no doubt insured. For how much?"

She paused, looked up at the ceiling as if thinking and finally answered in a small voice. "Seventy five thousand dollars."

I choked. Silence accompanied by eye rolls by the team. Octavius picked up on the conversation. "That's quite a substantial sum for a synthetic stone."

She gasped. "It's not synthetic. It's a natural diamond. Where did you get that idea?"

"From the jeweler who sold it to your husband. Mr. Alex. He has a shop here on the ship. He clearly recalls the transaction. It was one of a kind."

"I don't know him."

"You are aware that, although regarded as real, synthetic diamonds have a much lower resale value than their mined natural cousins."

"The insurance company accepted the valuation, issued the policy and we've been keeping up the premiums. I expect to be fully compensated."

"Assuming the necklace is not recovered."

"Of course assuming it's not recovered. But isn't that what you and ship's security team are trying to do? I don't understand where your questions are leading."

I decided to speak up. "We're just trying to get as full a profile of the situation as possible. These valuable thefts can often be complicated. We don't know who or how many individuals could be involved. Someone knew the lights would be off for a few minutes. Who and how? We don't believe it was an impulse act. It was planned by a knowledgeable party or parties. We're on guard for a repeat performance. Yours is not the only valuable jewelry on the ship. For example, Doctor Bear's wife, the Bearoness has quite a collection."

"Yes, I met her. She came to my assistance when I was assaulted. Lovely bear."

Octavius rose to his full height, startling the nanny goat. "Well, I think we've taken enough of your time. We'll be back when we have more news to report. We'll send your children back."

We got up to leave. The Frau left the laptop containing Ursula sitting unobtrusively on the tabletop. The goat didn't notice. We sent Carson and Cassidy back to the suite. Octavius, Lord David and I went to our respective elevators. The She-wolf walked down the passage way, paused at the lounge and sat.

The two siblings rushed into the suite. "How did it go?"

She replied, "They're suspicious. I don't like it. They're on to something. They know the diamond is synthetic and not worth what it's insured for. Carson, are you sure you have the necklace carefully hidden? I can't wear it any longer but I don't want to lose it. It does have great sentimental value."

"It's hidden among the props backstage in the theater. In with a bunch of dust covered costumes and jewelry. As soon as they decide to give up the search, I'll bring it back to you. I wish you'd get rid of the damned thing."

Cassidy bleated. "We need that diamond to stay stolen. I need that insurance money for college and my expenses. We can't bleed any more money from the company for a while. Too many of those unicorns are going belly up. They need fixing. That will be your job, Carson."

"I know my job, sister dear. Just shut up. I'm sick of catering to your demands. As Mama knows, the company's in trouble. You're going to have to tighten your belt a bit, my pet. A few less parties and cruises. You may even have to go to a less prestigious college or not at all. Won't that be a blow to your social climbing."

"You rotten skunk!"

They were interrupted by a knock on the door. Carson opened it. Frau Ilse was standing there. "Your pardon, Herr Carson. We forgot our laptop.

Each one of us thought the other had it. Oh, I see it. Over there on the table. Thank you again, Madame Caprine."

She strode in and with one sweeping motion took the computer, turned and left. As she exited, she could hear Cassidy saying. "God, that wolf is scary."

"So is that bear. The Dalmatian started out pleasant enough but he got insistent. I don't know why the meerkat was along but he did shed a little light on what they're up to."

Carson shook his head. "They're up to finding the diamond. That's what they're up to. I'm going to take a chance and move it from the theater back stage."

Chapter Twelve

The lost necklace has now been returned.
And the culprits have been badly burned.
On this hazardous run
The Octavians won.
Solar Sea's gratefulness has been earned.

Back at the Imperial Suite, Chief Security Officer Diomede waddled in, swinging a bright diamond necklace in his claw. The Albatross chuckled. "It was right where you said it would be, Doctor Bear. How did you know?"

"Deductive reasoning, Commander. The robber couldn't have gotten too far before the lights came on again. That's why I ordered up a thorough sweep of the theater."

"Yes, but you pinpointed it to the costumes."

"It seemed to be the most logical place. I'll share our discovery methods with you in a little while." He was not going to reveal Ursula 17 or her marvelous talents. That information was for Octavians only.

"Well, I guess I'll take the necklace down and show it to Mrs. Caprine. I'll still have to hold on to it as evidence, but she'll be delighted it's been found."

The Frau whispered to me. "I doubt it!"

Octavius held up a paw. "No don't do that yet. We still haven't found the culprit. Let's act as if the diamond is still missing. When the robbers discover the diamond isn't where he or she stashed it, they may give themselves away. We still have a few days on this cruise to ferret out the villains. Would you mind letting me keep the stone for a day or two. I realize it's important evidence."

He thought about it but finally agreed. "Please don't lose it."

"We'll keep it in the safe here in the suite along with the Bearoness' jewelry. We'll be very careful. We're going back down there. You may want to join us. "

Octavius rolled out a special safe we had brought on board. (*Never trust hotel or ship's room safes. Too many animals have access to them.*) He wouldn't put the diamond in there just yet. We copied the Caprines' conversation that Ursula had recorded on to a cell phone. The Bear called the Captain and Purser, played back the dialogue, explained the situation and invited them to join his team and the albatross at Luxury Deck Four, Suite Three A.

*****

Cassidy, Carson and Cassandra were in the suite. Carson had stolen *(no pun)* down to the theater backstage to check on the diamond and reassure his mother. He came rushing back in a panic. "It's gone. I tore the place apart but it's not there."

Cassidy moaned. "You careless fool. It was a stupid place to hide it. Some actor or performer probably found it."

"I didn't have enough time to hide it somewhere more secure and I didn't want to give the location away. Those security guys have been everywhere."

Cassandra was beside herself. "I want that necklace back. Yes, we'll collect the insurance but I want the diamond."

They were interrupted by a knock on the suite door. Cassidy bleated. "Oh, who's this? I'll send them away."

She opened the door and looked at a leonine face under a captain's brimmed cap. "Captain Lion, hello. What brings you here?"

"Hello, Ms. Caprine. May we come in?"

She giggled, "Of course, it's your ship. Mama, Carson. It's the Captain and he has some other animals with him."

Carson wasn't feeling sociable. "What's this all about, Captain? I think you know how upset my mother is."

"Yes, I do, Mr. Caprine. I'm afraid she's going to be more upset in just a few moments. I don't know if you've met our Chief Purser, Commander Gillian Greyhound. You're familiar with our Security Officer and of course, Doctor Octavius Bear and members of his Octavian team. Doctor Bear has something we want you to hear."

Octavius signaled to Frau Ilse and she pulled out her cell phone and played back the goats' recent conversations. Cassandra fainted. Cassidy broke out crying and Carson looked to the door but decided that wouldn't have been a good move. He decided to tough it out. "How dare you bug our suite and record our private discussion."

The Purser growled, "How dare you attempt to perpetrate insurance fraud and have ship security, our detectives and our staffs going crazy looking for a non-existent assailant and a diamond you had in your possession all this time. If this was England we'd have you up at least on charges for wasting police time. As it is, you're up against it for trying to pull off a high value scam. You're going to the brig, the three of you."

Cassidy wailed all the louder. Her mother woke back up just in time to hear the word 'brig' and promptly passed out again.

Carson looked at the Captain, "What do you plan on doing besides arresting us?'

"I don't know yet. I'd like to toss you over the side but you'd just land on the Cruise Center slip. We're holding on to the diamond and I'm calling our corporate office for guidance on how to handle this. We'll see what our executives and lawyers have to say. Meanwhile, your stay in this luxury suite is over. The brig is a lot less comfortable. I hope we don't have to cuff you. Commander Diomede, will you do the honors?"

Three members of the security staff took a leg each and hustled the trio out of the suite and down below decks.

The Captain turned to the Great Bear and said, "Not sure how to thank you, Doctor Bear. Between that Gladys Vaquero monster and these three, you and your team have had your paws full. Your folks pitched in and provided a lot of entertainment, too. Add that damn storm to the list and your retirement cruise has been anything but leisurely. For openers, Gillian, let's put together a real slap-up feast for the entire Octavian Group. Top of the line for everything."

"Let's also offer a free scuba and snorkel diving excursion to the Palancar Caves."

"I'm not sure you'll want to take advantage of it but I'm recommending to Corporate that we give you and your team an all expenses paid trip on any one of our cruises. Maybe next time you can get to enjoy yourselves without any more nonsense."

The Frau howled. "Not likely, Herr Captain. Not likely." She couldn't wait to tell Belinda and the Twins all about the day's events. The kids would love it. More material for *Bears at Sea*. Giselle, Otto, Howard. Jack and Chita would all be bummed out that they didn't get a shot at solving the Nonexistent Diamond Heist. But they weren't about to pass up a culinary celebration and diving excursion. Octavius and Belinda would probably pass on the free cruise although the Twins might push for it. The Bearoness had another bigger idea and she wanted to get together with Solar Seas Cruise Line Corporate Management as soon as the ship returned to Fort Lauderdale.

*****

Meanwhile, Cozumel beckoned.

A large van pulled up to the ship and Freddi Fox, the Social Directress directed all the Octavians who were up for a swim in the underwater paradise of Palancar to pile in. Harriet Hare, the ever-ready cruise social reporter was breathlessly poised to record the undersea frolics. Needless to say, the Twins were thrilled. More material for their games. Cameras at the ready.

*(Octavius and Bel elected to stay on the **SS SOLARWIND**. Chita and Jack, neither of whom were very fond of water also held back and organized a card game. The casino was closed. The Bearoness was looking forward to an afternoon of relaxing with a bowl or two of champagne. She would lead the ladies on a shopping expedition tomorrow. Octavius had managed to bring along a large jug of mead and intended to polish it off. Otto, a river otter, was in his element and persuaded Giselle to come along. The dogs and wolves always enjoyed a good splash or two.)*

After a short ride, the van pulled up at a docked dive boat and the group scrambled aboard. They divided up between snorkelers and scuba divers and took up the essential equipment. The Twins had hoped for a pair of jetskis or underwater scooters but discovered they were banned to protect the reef and its denizens. Oh, well, they could use bear power to propel themselves amid the fish, sharks and abundant sea turtles. But the coral was the star of the show. Not only was it beautiful, It was constructed in a fashion that allowed swim-throughs. A natural aquatic cathedral! Not quite the Great Barrier Reef but close enough for great fun and enjoyment.

After several hours of exploring and cavorting with the underwater vertebrates, the Octavians were ready to go back to the ship where a sumptuous banquet was being prepared. Tired but excited, they prepared to be feted.

*****

Promptly at seven they entered a large conference room that had been laid out on one end for a formal dinner. The ladies, led by Belinda, had decided to dress up. In spite of or maybe because of the recent diamond fiasco, jewelry was in heavy evidence. The males stuck with their usual garb, if any. The Twins, came loaded down with video equipment. Harriet Hare had her recorder at the ready. The Captain and ship's commanders, wearing their dress uniforms, circulated with the party goers.

Members of the wait staff moved about in the open space offering all forms of liquid refreshment and nibbles. After the group had been sufficiently lubricated, Freddi Fox rang a chime and said. "Ladies and gentlebeasts, please be seated. You'll find place cards with you names on them." At each space, next to the exquisite china, glassware and cutlery, was a small model of the **SS SOLARWIND**. "

The Captain tapped his glass for attention. The Twins fired up their video cameras and Harriet had her recorder going. "Ladies and Gentlebeasts. I am very pleased to welcome all of you to our special recognition dinner. As you are all well aware, this has been a somewhat trying voyage. I won't repeat all the issues that occurred but suffice it say that while cruise ship crews are used to unusual events, this trip was a bit more unusual than we anticipated. Let us simply say that **SS SOLARWIND's** maiden voyage has been quite eventful." *(See Book 18- The Bear Faced Liar, to complete the story.)*

"I and my Staff are extremely grateful for the outstanding assistance all of you have provided. I hope your undersea adventure today and this dinner will provide you with some sense of our thanks. Let us hope in the remaining days here in Cozumel and on our trip back to Fort Lauderdale, you will have the opportunity to simply relax and enjoy yourselves here on this wonderful ship."

"My special gratitude to Doctor Octavius Bear and his gracious mate, the Bearoness. You will be remembered fondly by our crew and the management of Solar Seas Cruise lines. Now, enough of me. Please enjoy your meal."

Octavius rose to his full nine foot height and held up a glass filled with who knows what. "Captain, thank you so much for your hospitality. As I think you know, we Octavians live for excitement. *(laughs from the group)* We have had an ample supply while on this voyage. Here's to you, your crew and this great ship. Long may she sail peacefully and in calm waters." *(standing applause.)*

The twins dove into their appetizers and the party went into full swing. Laughter, conversations, clinking glassware, background music. None of this made its way down to the ship's brig or to a jail cell in Houston. The noises there were different.

*****

106

Next morning, the last day **SS SOLARWIND** would be in Cozumel, Belinda and Freddi organized a shopping spree for the ladies at the island's plentiful duty free shops in San Miguel. The twins were busy working up avatars for their Virtual Reality version of *Bears at Sea*. Several of the males were sleeping in after a night of overdoing it. A few of the females passed on the shops for the same reason.

Octavius went to the bridge seeking out the Captain. He caught him in his conference room conferring with the Purser. They were on a Zoom session with members of the Solar Seas Corporate Office. He waved the Great Bear in and announced his presence to the executives. Wally Wapiti, the CEO took a moment to thank Octavius for all of his assistance. He added, "I gather the Bearoness has a business proposition she wants to discuss with us. About her Scottish resort. She's a formidable lady."

The Bear laughed. "My wife has taken a fusty castle overrun by her in-laws and converted it back to the luxury resort the original laird intended it to be. She tossed them out and used her late husband's wealth to create Polar Paradise and Bearonial Enterprises. It's a roaring success. *(no pun)* In addition to being a glamorous show business talent, she's a commercial genius. I'd listen to what she has to say, if I were you."

"Oh, we intend to. We have a meeting scheduled for her arrival at Fort Lauderdale. Right now, we're trying to figure how to deal with those larcenous goats."

Also on the screen were Bill Beaver, former Senior VP of Sales and Marketing, recently promoted to COO; Corporate Attorney Emilia Emu and Corporate Security Officer Pablo Puma.

The lawyer spoke, "We've been in contact with the Caprine's insurance company. They've immediately cancelled the policy on the diamond and kept the remainder of the premium in lieu of damages. They insure a number of the Caprine Associates officers and board and are reluctant to press charges. It seems the company is in financial trouble and a scandal wouldn't help any. I personally would like to throw the book at them. Pablo agrees with me. Chiselers! They certainly had the whole ship and your folks all wound up. That daughter sounds like a real spoiled brat."

Bill Beaver, who still seemed to be wearing his marketing hat said, "We don't need that kind of agita. Too many incidents on the **SS SOLARWIND** already She's our new flagship, for goodness sake. We don't want her known as the crime ship. Although some weirdos might be attracted to that, I don't think the plutocrats who can afford our luxury suites would be enthralled."

Wally Wapiti agreed. "The insurance company stood to take a big hit and they decided against pressing charges. The goats didn't actually commit fraud."

The Emu snorted. "Through no fault of their own! It was just a matter of time and opportunity. Those grifters! They hid the necklace and were certainly planning to defraud the insurers before Doctor Bear's people caught them out. What do you think, Octavius."

"Although this ship took a hit from their chicanery, the insurance company is the major potential victim. If they're not willing to sue or press charges, I think you folks should keep them in the brig until we reach Lauderdale. Refuse to return the diamond and release them until they pay their bill in full and sign a non-disclosure agreement promising not to talk about the whole affair. That stupid doe might try to make a sensational story out of it for the scandal sheets."

The Captain interrupted. "I can't keep them prisoner if no one is going to press charges."

"You know that and we know that but they don't know that. Let them sweat a little. Excuse me. I have a date with a keg of mead."

Chapter Thirteen

On its way back to Fort Lauderdale
At the end of its maidenly sail,
SOLARWIND needs repair
But the tourists don't care.
Fun and wild entertainment prevail.

The **SS SOLARWIND** pulled away from the Punta Langosta Terminal at Cozumel and moved out into the open waters heading for Fort Lauderdale and much needed repairs. The passengers scrambled about the ship in a flurry of activity trying to squeeze every minute of fun and relaxation out of the last two days. Both the Lido and VIP pools were packed. The lounges, bars and restaurants overflowed. All manner of pizza was consumed by the ton and the casino echoed with noises from gamblers and hyperactive slot machines. The shops were super busy. Screaming kids, kittens and puppies took to the rides and game boards. Security was busy locating missing youngsters and the occasional drunk. Thank goodness, the Vaqueros were gone.

On the bridge, the command staff were preparing for their return to Home Port. The Staff Captain and Purser were entering their reports on the ship's computer while the Captain and First Officer monitored the vessel's automatic pilot, engines and the weather. Clear skies predicted for the next few days along the route. With any luck, the rest of the trip would be uneventful.

So what befell our villains?

At the FBI Field Office, Gladys Vaquero's lawyers were unable to get her out on bail due to the extreme nature of the crime for which she was charged. She was also designated a flight risk and had to surrender her passport. They entered a plea of self defense but the surveillance tapes plainly showed her deliberately drowning and stabbing her husband repeatedly. She was transferred to a Federal lockup where she is awaiting trial and driving her jailers crazy with her constant screams, moans, moos and complaints.

The Caprine family was a different story. Cassandra was just relieved that they were being released from the brig and the insurance company was not pressing charges. She was comforted by the return of the necklace but found herself and the company in deep financial trouble. Several of the board members had bailed out as one unicorn after another rolled over and died.

Carson found himself without a job to go to. He was lucky he wasn't in jail on the mainland. Cassidy was bereft. They could no longer afford her posh college or her expensive lifestyle. She might even have to work. OMG! What would her friends say? She protested about having to sign the non-disclosure agreement but was finally convinced that writing a confession for a scandal tabloid wasn't such a hot idea.

While she was loath to part with it, Cassandra tried to sell the necklace but nobody would touch it. Mr. Alex had spread the word in the jewelry community. The diamond would go into a family safe where it was doomed to remain, never to reappear.

*****

The final night passed without incident and the Octavians were taken up with getting ready to fly back to the Bear's Lair In Cincinnati and then for some, on to Polar Paradise in the Shetlands.

The great Bear, Belinda and I made a pilgrimage to the bridge to thank the Captain and Command Staff for what was, on balance, a delightful trip. He reciprocated and said to Belinda, "Wally Wapiti will be on Zoom in the morning. I understand you two have some business to transact." She grinned. He looked at Octavius who only smiled back.

Next morning, as they glided into the Port Everglades-Fort Lauderdale Ship Terminal, the Bearoness was in the bridge conference room with the Captain on a video connection with the execs of Solar Seas Cruise Lines. She was accompanied by Octavius, an Ursula and me. "Good morning, Mr. Wapiti, lady and gentlebeasts. I have a proposal to make to you. As I think you know, I am in the resort business and own a large, highly successful leisure facility in the Shetlands. Polar Paradise. I want to grow it. Octavius and I would like to invest. perhaps heavily, in your cruise line but on one condition."

"Intriguing, milady. What do you have in mind?"

"In addition to the Caribbean, how would you like to take your ships North. The North Atlantic and the North Sea. The UK, Scandinavia, Germany, Northern Ireland and Scotland. Linked up to our resort in the Shetlands. There's a major holiday market among cold loving animals. Not just polar bears. As you know, the number of species that live in frigid conditions is amazing. Let's build a vacation service for them. You provide the ships and manage the routes. I'll provide finances, a terminal and an expanded resort, for starters. Of course, we'll need to develop several ports of call in the European countries but my husband and I are not without influence and resources."

Bill Beaver, the new COO and ex-marketeer was fascinated. "Can you work up a proposal, Bearoness?"

"Already have. And a business plan. Octavius is on board and Maury Meerkat is an astute promoter. I'll send it to you. Hopefully, we can keep the criminals out and the good guys in. Talk to you soon. We have to get off your ship" She laughed and cut the connection. Ursula had it all down.

In the office, Wapiti chuckled. "Amazing female. He's amazing, too. Owns and controls UUI. A gazillionaire. Sounds like a ready-made market. We do have the ships. Not the **SOLARWIND**. At least, not yet. Some of our smaller units or superyachts. "

Back on the ship, Octavius looked at me and we both laughed. So much for retirement.

*****

Among the crowd waiting for the debarking passengers, was a mob of reporters. Octavius was livid. News of the tropical storm, malware attack and murder had all hit the media outlets. The teams had managed to keep the necklace affair confidential although one or two of the ship's security unit had blabbed some but not all of the details. The goats had been released but were incommunicado.

I had an idea and called the Purser. We made an arrangement. Octavius and Belinda would be housed in a large shipping container and hauled out of the cargo hold and transported by truck to the airport and the waiting Otter. The plane, not the animal. Hardly dignified or comfortable but effective. The rest of us dodged the journalists and rode a shuttle bus to the airport.

The DHC-6-300 Twin Otter stood in the General Aviation area at FLL Airport awaiting its complement of passengers for the trip back to Cincinnati and the Bear's Lair. The Flying Tigers arrived early and had seen to the refueling. They were going through their external and internal checklists when the shuttle drove up to the flight line and unloaded the Twins, Giselle, Chita, Wyatt, Ilse, Bearyl and Bearnice, Jaguar Jack, Lord David, Dancing Dan, Howard and Otto and of course me, Maury. *(along with the omnipresent Ursulas.)*

Otto patted the fuselage of his namesake aircraft as they placed their luggage in the stowage compartment. "Good old girl. Ready whenever we are. I'm glad I don't have to 'zap' back to Ohio. Takes a lot of energy and adrenaline. It's bad enough I have to make three quantum jumps in the next few days. Howard and his exoplanets."

Octavius and Belinda arrived with their baggage a bit worse for wear from their trip in the shipping container but he avoided the press. He hated reporters. Chita and I loved them but he's the boss.

The heavily loaded plane taxied to the flight line and waited to be released and vectored out of Lauderdale air space. Cruise ships are fun but it was time for a little Cincinnati terra firma to say nothing of the Bear's Lair comforts. The Shetlands denizens would be lofted on the Concorde back to Polar Paradise.

All this was faithfully recorded by the Ursulas. McTavish and Arabella were up to their ursine ears developing a standard and Virtual Reality game and adventure. ***Bears at Sea!***

Epilogue

Their retirement plan slowly pales
Since Belinda has plans for more sails.
There'll be more Bears at Sea
So, dear readers, feel free
To come back for some more of our tales. (tails?)

Six months later:

Belinda was stretched out on a banquette, champagne bowl in paw in the Polar Paradise lounge. She was thinking of what had happened to their pseudo retirement. Most of the Octavians had chosen to join Octavius and the Bearoness at the Shetlands castle to unwind after their sea-borne adventures on the **SS SOLARWIND**. What was supposed to be a relaxing 14 day cruise had turned out to be a crime filled, storm ridden series of adventures. Their year-long experimental retirement sabbatical was turning out to be anything but. It was best described by Frau Schuylkill: "trouble follows them around like their tails."

Nevertheless, Belinda, the astute business sow, had entered into negotiations with the Solar Seas Cruise Line to open up a North Atlantic itinerary with Polar Paradise as a port of call. They worked out a combination tour and resort stay package. Aimed at cold weather aficionados like polar bears, arctic foxes, reindeer, snow leopards, musk oxen, caribou and surprise, even penguins, their research predicted a lively market. The cruise company had agreed to initiate a bi-monthly voyage visiting the British, Scottish, Northern Irish, Scandinavian and Arctic climes.

She, in turn, set about constructing a docking facility and expanded heliport adjacent to the castle suitable for one of the line's smaller but luxurious ships – The North Wind. Further south, the city of Abeardeen was investigating whether to build a similar facility along its shoreline. Negotiations were afoot with several Northern European countries.

Work on the cruise center was proceeding apace and supplying temporary employment to a substantial population of Scottish crafts specialists and laborers. Harold, the Sea Otter, was reshaping the shore line and rehousing the castle's pleasure craft. The villages of Baltasound and Unst were invaded by newcomers but enjoying a major spike in revenues. The Lion and Unicorn pub opened an inn, hostel and restaurant for the workers. They would be converted eventually for cruise line day trippers who chose not to stay at or couldn't afford the luxurious castle resort. Fiona, former manager of the Lion and Unicorn lounge at Polar Paradise was now the director of Lion and Unicorn Properties and Ventures.

So much for the Bearoness retiring. Bearonial Enterprises were prospering. She had promoted Dougal, former castle resort manager, to project director for the expansion - Operation North Star. Ms. Fairbearn took over running the castle, itself. Lord David and Dancing Dan took up the resort's business operations and Chita is now also handling the publicity and marketing for the enterprise. The name Polar Paradise was being recast to reflect the near Arctic location as opposed to catering primarily to Polar Bears. However, the white ursines remain a major segment of the resort's clientele.

The Twins, working with Chita, Condo and the staff at the Hexagon are busy creating Social Media, Virtual Reality, Metaverse, games and entertainment apps in support of the new endeavors as well as exploiting the expanding digital marketplace. Byzz continues to enhance the miraculous Ursulas who increasingly contribute to all the Octavian and Bearonial endeavors.

The Great Bear has fully reestablished his command of UUI and I, his faithful second am doing what seconds do in addition to running my growing talent agency. Otto and Giselle are now a sensational theater and TV act making appearances in major cities and venues including, of course, Polar Paradise. Bearyl and Bearnice are winning critical raves and awards and have more gigs than they can handle. Lepi has become a matinee idol. Belinda herself, with my help is supervising the aqua theater and live shows.

Howard and Marlin have been working with NASA and the Spider Web Telescope Authority and have uncovered a number of interesting exoplanets for future exploration.

In spite of all this change and apparent progress, the Octavians carry on their crime fighting activities with the Frau and Colonel taking the lead but calling on the rest of us as necessary. Jaguar Jack is a major contributor and Huntley occasionally sheds his butler's livery to chase bad guys. And of course, detecting is Octavius' first love. He recently heard from Chief Inspector Bruce Wallaroo and Tilda Roo and is about to take another run Down Under.

In addition to piloting the Great Bear's Air Force, Ben and Gal, the Flying Tigers are working with Octavius' UUI Aviation Division in developing a new ultrasonic transport with tolerable auditory booms. However, Belinda will never give up her beloved Concorde SST. They're also developing a drone-based air taxi for moving around UUI properties.

Time marches on. With one of the clone sheep lounge waitresses (Dolly, Molly, Holly or Polly) refilling her champagne bowl, Belinda sat and thought. She was facing up to another issue. Her father, Polonius Polar Black, US senator from Alaska was on his way to Polar Paradise to visit her. She had only recently become aware of him. Polar paters have a habit of disappearing from or worse yet attacking their offspring. Her mother, Beartha Black had died years ago, drowning in an accident on an ice floe. Who was he and what did he want? He probably knew she was incredibly wealthy and was looking for a substantial contribution for his election campaign. "Lots of luck, Dad. Where have you been all my life?"

She mentioned it to Octavius. His reaction was, "Tell him to get lost." That's what she planned to do.

The End

Bears at Sea

BOOK 19 of THE CASEBOOKS OF OCTAVIUS BEAR

About the Author

Harry DeMaio is a ***nom de plume*** of Harry B. DeMaio, successful author of several books on Information Security and Business Networks as well as the nineteen-volume ***Casebooks of Octavius Bear.*** His four volume series, ***Sherlock Holmes and the Glamorous Ghost*** has been very well received. He is also a published author of pastiches for Belanger Books and the MX Sherlock Holmes series. A retired business executive, former consultant, information security specialist, elected official, private pilot, disk jockey and graduate school adjunct professor, he whiles away his time traveling and writing preposterous books, articles and stories.

He has appeared on many radio and TV shows and is an accomplished, frequent public speaker.

Former New York City natives, he and his extremely patient and helpful wife, Virginia, live in Cincinnati (and several other parallel universes.) They have two sons, Mark, living in Scottsdale, Arizona and Andrew. in Cortlandt Manor, New York, both of whom are quite successful and quite normal, thus putting the lie to the theory that insanity is hereditary.

Comments are welcome. Positive or negative, His skin is thick. Of course, positive is better.

His e-mail is hdemaio@zoomtown.com

You can also find him on Facebook.

His website is www.tavighostbooks.com

His books are available on Amazon, Barnes and Noble, the Book Depository and other fine bookstores as well as directly from MX Publishing and Belanger Books.

Milton Keynes UK
Ingram Content Group UK Ltd.
UKHW050622250923
429338UK00011B/530